Her Man, His Savage 2

Tina J

Copyright 2017

This novel is a work of fiction. Any resemblances to actual events, real people, living or dead, organizations, establishments or locales are products of the author's imagination. Other names, characters, places, and incidents are used fictionally.

More Books by Tina J

A Thin Line Between Me & My Thug 1-2
I Got Luv for My Shawty 1-2
Kharis and Caleb: A Different kind of Love 1-2
Loving You is a Battle 1-3
Violet and the Connect 1-3
You Complete Me
Love Will Lead You Back
This Thing Called Love
Are We in This Together 1-3
Shawty Down to Ride For a Boss 1-3
When a Boss Falls in Love 1-3
Let Me Be The One 1-2
We Got That Forever Love
Ain't No Savage Like The One I got 1-2
A Queen & Hustla 1-2 (collab)
Thirsty for a Bad Boy 1-2
Hasaan and Serena: An Unforgettable Love 1-2
We Both End Up With Scars
Are We in this Together 1-3
Caught up Luvin a beast 1-3
A Street King & his Shawty 1-2
I Fell for the Wrong Bad Boy 1-2 (collab)
Addicted to Loving a Boss 1-3
I need that Gangsta Love 1-2 (collab)
Still Luvin' a Beast 1-2
I Wanna Love You 1-2
When She's Bad, I'm Badder 1-3
Her Man, His Savage 1-2

Previously...

Zander

"Where is she Unique?" I asked when she opened the door. I know Mike wanted to ask me to see if she knew where Ashanti was, but he didn't. I planned on it, however, I had to mentally get ready to see her. I was still in love with her, no doubt, but she did some fucked up shit at the dinner.

"Where's who?" I moved past her and checked the entire house.

"The Ashanti bitch."

"Zander, don't call my cousin a bitch."

"Why not? She tried to kill my brothers' girl."

"I know." She put her head down and closed the door.

"So again. Where is she?"

"Honestly, I don't know."

"Don't play with me."

"I'm serious. After she shot the Gianna chick, your brother literally, knocked her out. I threw water on her face and

4

she jumped up. She seemed ok and told me to leave and we'd speak tomorrow. I didn't hear from her and went by to check on her because I knew your brother was gonna kill her. When I got there, she was gone."

"You do know Mike's gonna kill her." She nodded. We both stood there, not saying a word.

"Zander, I want to apologize for the dinner."

"Unique, I'm good." I walked to the door and she stopped me.

"I didn't terminate the baby." I stopped and smirked without her seeing. I didn't want her to get rid of the baby and I said the shit, because of my anger. She came and stood in front of me.

"Baby, I'm so sorry. Misfit asked me to go to the dinner, to feel her out. I was in my feelings because he was loving on her and I'm not used to seeing him happy with anyone. Zander." She turned my face to hers.

"It was disrespectful to both of you and I'm sorry. I swear, on our baby that you're the man I want." Her hands went to my buckle.

5

"Unique."

"Hmmm."

"You don't have to. Oh damnnnnn." I stared down, placed my hand on her head and enjoyed watching her suck all my babies. She stood up, removed her shirt and I looked down.

"How far are you?" I placed my hand on her belly. She used to have washboard abs and now, there's a small pouch.

"Two and a half months."

"You know he's gonna be a junior."

"We don't even know if it's a boy." I lifted her up.

"Oh, it's a boy." I kissed her neck and walked to the bedroom. By the time, I got all her clothes off, my dick was busting through my jeans. He wanted to feel inside her.

"Ah shitttttt ma. I missed being in you." I went as slow as possible but still came fast.

"My bad."

"You better had cum fast." I started laughing. She climbed on top of me and the two of us made up for lost time. She was laying in front of me and I was dosing off.

"Zander."

6

"Yea babe."

"There's something I need to talk to you about." I opened my eyes and stared at her. She was so damn beautiful.

"What's up?" My phone started ringing.

"Go head and answer it."

"It's fine Unique. What's up?" She opened her mouth to speak and stopped when my phone rang again.

"It may be important." I reached for it.

"Yo."

"She's awake and not taking it well, after hearing about her legs."

"I'm on my way." I hung up and stood to grab my clothes.

"Everything ok?"

"Yea. Gianna just woke up." I wasn't telling Unique much about her condition, just in case, she is still in contact with Ashanti.

"Oh ok. Zander, I'm really sorry about the chaos."

"Don't let it happen again."

"I won't." She came over and kissed me. I was ready to go back inside the bedroom. However, my brother needed me. He's probably stressing himself out. I hopped in my car and drove to the hospital. I'm sure it's gonna be a long day.

****

"You ready?" Mike asked as we made our way into the hotel.

"Hold on."

"Hey." It was Unique calling.

"How long are you gonna be out? I really wanna speak to you about something?" Whatever it is, she had to tell me, must be weighing on her because this is the third time, she brought it up.

"A few hours. I have a meeting in a couple of hours and I promise to come straight to your house, when I'm done."

"A meeting at work?" She questioned.

"Something like that. Remember the guy, I told you about who called me from my last job?"

"Yea."

"He asked me to come work for him today."

8

"Ummmm ok. I'll see you later."

"You ok Unique?"

"Yea, I will be. I have to go too." She hung up and usually, I'd call back to check on her but Mike and I were getting ready.

"I wanna get this shit done and get to Gia. She's been cursing the staff out and trying to walk on her own." Mike said and shook his head.

Gianna had temporary paralysis and she's been trying to gain feeling in her legs on her own. The doctor told her, the feeling will come when its time, but her stubborn ass ain't making shit easy for them at the hospital. Mike, hired extra physical therapists for her, so she could do therapy more than once a day. She was determined by all means to get up walking. That and the fact, she wants to kill Ashanti, pregnant and all. Mike asked her to wait, until after she had the baby and she flipped the hell out on him. He couldn't win for losing right now, with her.

I picked up my MK-12 Rifle and Mike pulled his MK-11 rifle out the bag. Both of these rifles, are sniper guns and

9

used mainly by the military. But with a man like Javier as your boss, it's never hard to get your hands on the good shit. They were both black and we had, hella ammunition.

The two people we were looking for, only needed to be disabled. However, in my eyes, if you're trying to terminate competition, why play with them? Kill they ass and move on. Leaving them alive, will only make room for retaliation.

It was now 9:45 and the meeting is supposed to start at 10 am sharp. We were in position and getting ready for whatever. Someone opened the window a little wider and gave a thumbs up. An amateur would assume, he could see us, but we knew he was giving us the ok. I put my hand on the trigger and waited for my target to arrive.

"Yo, dude looks mad familiar." Mike said when a guy walked in. I took a look and he was right, unfortunately, I didn't know who he was and gave zero fucks. I wanted this job to be over, so I can check on my girl and kid.

"Its time." I told my brother when my alarm went off. I had it set to 9:58.

At exactly 9:59, my target walked in with the hoodie on, jeans and sneakers. I guess this so-called ghost, really didn't wanna be seen. Something was very familiar about my target, but again, I ignored it and waited for the door to open. The door opened and like Javier said, there was a commotion, when Mike's target walked in.

SWISH! SWISH! SWISH! SWISH! Is the only sound that was heard in our hotel room. The guns were quiet and the bullets sounded like a bug, flying past your head.

"Look at those bodies drop. Bro, we the shit." Mike said and we started laughing. The two targets hit the floor and you saw motherfuckers going crazy. We started packing our shit up to leave. There was no need to watch the rest, because we knew the outcome.

Mike and I, wiped everything down, put the hoodies on our head, with the dark sunglasses and stepped out the room. It didn't take us long to get downstairs and to the black van, Javier brought. We hopped in and drove it to the chop shop, changed clothes, jumped in our own clothes and went our separate ways.

11

I went to my condo, took a shower and headed over to see Unique. I was getting in my car, when her friend Elsie pulled up and jumped out. I don't even know how she knew where I lived. She came over and gave me a hug, with tears falling down her face. I moved her back and asked what happened.

"Unique's been shot."

"WHAT?" I started panicking. I know Chanelle didn't try to fucking kill her.

"Misfit, called and told me to come get you because he didn't have your number. Zander, he said its really bad and she may not make it." My phone started ringing and it was Mike.

"Yo, someone shot Unique. Meet me at the hospital."

"Bro, I'm here and Gia is missing."

"WHAT THE FUCK?" I told him we'd be right there and to meet me down in the emergency room.

I damn near fell out the car, when we got there because I didn't wait for Elsie to stop. Mike was waiting for me outside. I ran in, and the hospital had mad niggas in the waiting area. I mean, ruthless looking niggas and then I saw two older people,

12

I'm assuming are her parents, Misfit and their daughter. I started to go ask the nurse what was going on but he stopped me.

"They have Unique in the back."

"Is she ok? What happened to her?" I was nervous as hell.

"We were at a meeting and she got shot."

Misfit

"What are you gonna do? She loves you." Ronald asked me in the phone, as I prepared myself to take out the woman, I fell in love with.

"What's love gotta do with it?" I stepped out the car and walked up slowly. Neither of them paid attention to their surroundings. I stood by the truck and picked up my vibrating phone.

"Yo!" I whispered on the line.

"Bro, where you at?" Shafee said in the phone. I moved it from my ear and looked at the time. It was 9:45 and I only had ten minutes to get there. I told him, I'd be right there. I pointed my gun at Krista and had my finger on the trigger.

"You choosing that grimy nigga over me?" I heard B-Huff say.

"Brian."

Brian? I know this isn't the nigga who hurt her. Now, I see why she didn't wanna tell me. *Fuck that!* As her man, she had the responsibility to inform me.

"I'm in love with him." I pulled my arm back and leaned against the truck. Could I kill her? I stepped away and went over to the warehouse. I'll deal with her later and if it has to be with death, then so be it.

I parked at the warehouse and went inside, only to find, everyone there, except K and Shafee. How the hell, he rushing me and his ass ain't here. I asked Champ where he was and he had no idea either. I took a seat next to him and looked down at my phone. Krista, sent me a text asking me to come by. How she texting me, with the nigga in her face? I put my phone up when K walked in. The black hoodie covered her and I could see in her face, how tired she was. Yup, K is a woman, a savage really.

A minute later, this fuck nigga walked in and all of us, stood up and pointed our guns at him. I just saw him with Krista. How did he get here so fast and why was he here? K, of

15

course went off because he was late and just as she turned around to tell is his purpose, her body dropped and so did his.

I ran over to her and she had blood coming out but I couldn't tell you where, because of the big hoodie she wore. K always wore this hoodie to meetings because it had a bullet proof vest under it. Its also to keep people from knowing who she was, if they were watching from the outside. What I didn't understand is, how she was bleeding with the vest on. Instead of trying to check it out, I carried her out the warehouse and Champ drove or should I say, sped to the hospital.

When we got there, Champ ran in and came out with a couple of nurses, and a doctor who had a gurney. They placed her on top and ran inside. There was so much blood on me, I went in the bathroom to wash myself off. I came out and Champ was walking in with an extra shirt. I still had blood on my jeans but at least my shirt was clear of it.

I made a phone call to her parents and then to Elsie. I had her go get her man, Zander and bring him here. Did I forget to mention that K, is Unique? They are the same person, but we'll get to that later. Of course, she was hysterical on the phone. I had to calm her down, just so she wouldn't crash on the way in.

"What the fuck happened?" Shafee came in with some guy.

"Where were you?"

"I was doing something for K. Or should I say bringing him to her. Riley, this is Misfit. Misfit, this is Riley. He's B-Huff's brother and has been working with us to get him."

"WHAT?"

"Him and K have been in contact with one another. He's the reason B-Huff was at the meeting in the first place."

"I'm lost."

"Let me explain." I walked behind him to a secluded area.

"K and I go way back." I looked at him.

"Not like that. I know, who you are Misfit, and wouldn't dare think about trying anything with her." I nodded. At least, he knew boundaries. K may not be my woman anymore, but she was in my life for a very long time.

"Her dad is the one who found me. See, B-Huff is my birth brother but he's no brother of mine."

"What you mean?"

"B-Huff is my younger brother who didn't wanna see me shine. What I'm saying is, the empire my father left, was given to me. I ran it with an iron fist and made sure not to overstep my boundaries. Meaning, don't bite off more than I can chew, or the hand who fed me, which back then, was Mr. Buffalo." I stood there with my arms folded.

"Long story short, Brian, wasn't happy with the BOSS status I had and did everything in his power to get rid of me; including giving me up to the cops."

"Say word!"

"Word. My brother is not only a certified snitch but has been trying to sleep with Unique, in hopes of joining forces with her. You didn't know, but they've been speaking on the phone a lot, but he had no idea she was K. Not knowing it, he fed her a lot of information. He tried relentlessly to bed her but again, she wasn't having it. His baby mama caught him on the phone with Unique, which is why, she left him. He had been cheating on her so much, it was the final straw."

"You're telling me, Krista knows Unique?"

"I'm not sure she knew who she was in the beginning, but if that's your woman now, I'm sure she put two and two together. I mean, how many Unique's are out here?" *I wonder why she never said anything to me about it.*

"I had my people's following him. When they told me where he was, I planned on making an entrance and taking him out."

"Well, looks like someone else had him on a list because him and Unique were shot, and we don't know by who."

"That's weird." He gave me a confusing look.

"Why you say that?"

"Because he barely had any enemies. The only other person who could've had a hit on him, is Javier and he's been off the grid for a very long time."

"Who the hell is Javier?"

"Shitttttt. He's one of the most notorious drug lords out there, with probably two of the best hit men ever. I mean, if he's out the game, they most likely are too. Him and my brother never had beef, so it's confusing me too."

"You think he'd put a hit on K?"

"That's the thing. He hasn't been active in a very long time, therefore; I can't say yes. However, if you're telling me a hit came from outside the warehouse, then it's possible. I will say this though. If he went out and recruited the two niggas he used to have, there's more names on the list, so plan for more funerals." He excused himself and went in the bathroom. I noticed Unique's parents coming in and some of the guys on our team.

"How is she?" Her mom asked.

"We don't know yet. She had the hoodie on but there was still a lot of blood." Her father slammed his hand against the wall.

"This was a fucking set up."

"Calm down honey."

"Don't tell me to calm down, when my daughter is in there shot up." She smacked the shit outta him and all of us turned our head. We didn't wanna seem disrespectful by watching.

"You don't raise your voice at me motherfucker. I told you about that shit before. Unique is my daughter too and right now, we need to stay calm until we figure out what's going on. You in here acting a damn fool and any of these niggas could be the one who shot her." I loved Unique's mom but when she got beside herself, I wanted to knock the shit outta her.

21

"Ma, really. Misfit, me or Champ, could be the one?"

"Oh boy, shut up. They know I'm not talking about them. Well, Misfit does have a new bitch now, so you never know."

"Listen here, Mrs. Buffalo." I stood in front of her. I could see her pops on the side of me.

"Your daughter and I, both have someone else, so don't come for me. Regardless, of that, you know, I would never put my hands on her, or try to kill her. She is the mother of my daughter."

"Psst." She tried to wave me off.

"As far as my woman, don't call her a bitch or worry about who I'm sticking my dick in. As long as my daughter, your granddaughter is ok, that's all you need to concern yourself with, when it comes to me."

"Let's go bro." Shafee moved me away from her. I saw the smirk on his father's face. I know y'all may think, I'm bugging by speaking to her that way, but she gets under my skin all the time and I have to let her know. It's not just me either. She does all of us like this and once we put her in her place, she shuts the fuck up, like she's doing now.

"Yo, I almost laughed in her face. You know, I can't keep a straight face when you and moms go at it." Shafee ain't shit.

"She lucky, she's your mom because I would've already slid her ass across the damn hospital floor."

"I know. Go get Angel out the car. The nanny just brought her." I looked at him. Why did the nanny have his number?

"I only hit it once." I gave him the side eye.

"Ok damn. I've been fucking the nanny for a year now." I fell out laughing.

This nigga is a nut and will stick his dick in anyone. The nanny is thirty, with an ok body and she's a Mexican American. He loved Hispanics but damn, did it have to be our nanny? She is very good with Angel and I know once Shafee fucks up, she'll quit. And I'm making him find a new one, if she does. I walked back in with Angel and a few minutes later, so did Zander. He looked stressed the fuck out. I guess, it's time to tell him what happened.

Zander

I ran into the emergency room and saw a lot of people, including Misfit and others. He came over to me and I asked what happened. When he told me, Unique was shot at a meeting; Mike and I looked at one another. There's no way, she was at the meeting we hit up. I didn't see any females in the warehouse, and I know my brother wouldn't have shot her, if he saw her. I need to find out what meeting she was at, before I drove myself crazy.

"What meeting was she at?" Misfit gave me a crazy look.

"Did Unique ever tell you who she was?" He questioned and some other guy, that resembled her, came over.

"What you mean, who she is?"

"Hmph." He said and gave me a weird look.

"Unique is, how should I put this." He had his hand rubbing over his head. Whatever he was about to tell me, had

25

to be weighing on him. I walked over to a corner with him and Mike, was right behind me. Misfit, surveyed the area to make sure no one was listening.

"Unique's father is an ex- kingpin, slash savage."

"Say what now?" I had to make sure I heard him correctly.

"Anyway, he passed the empire down to his daughter because Shafee here, didn't want it. Long story short, Unique is a BOSS, and any other violent person you can think of. She has more bodies under her, than her pops and people fear her." So, the shit Chanelle said is true about her being crazy.

"You're telling me, my girl, is a savage?"

"Exactly!"

"What the fuck?"

"However, they don't know who she is." I turned around to face him.

"If they don't know who she is, how are the fearing her?"

26

"They don't know her as Unique. They know her as K." The color had to have drained from my face.

"Come again." Mike said, what I was thinking.

"Her full name is Unique Kaye Buffalo. We use her middle name, to keep people from finding out who she is."

"Bro, you fucking my sister and don't know her name." Shafee said.

"Fuck you. I know her name but I didn't know she was out in the streets. She told me, she owns her business and that's it. I wonder if it's what she wanted to tell me."

"What you mean?'

"She kept saying, she had to talk to me but something always came up. I was supposed to see her today, after.-" I stopped myself.

"After what?"

"Nothing. I need to know if she lost the baby."

"BABY!" Both of them shouted.

"Yea baby. You know, when you have sex with no condom, a baby comes out of it." Misfit shook his head and her brother walked away and to his parents.

"Mike."

"I know man." We both walked outside to speak privately.

"FUCK! How did I not know who she was?" I had my hands on my head.

"Mannn, she was on some secretive shit."

"This is a lot." We stood there in silence.

"You gonna be good because I have to go to security and see if I can get the tapes. Somebody took my girl."

"Oh shit. Yea go head. You want me to come?"

"Nah. Handle this and we'll link up later." He walked back in the hospital. I leaned on the wall, with my leg up and head resting against it. I pulled my phone out my pocket and called the only person, I knew, who could tell me what the fuck is going on.

"Hola! Good job and your money has been transferred over." I knew it did because the alert came on my phone, five minutes after the hit was done.

"Yo, what the fuck is really good?"

"I'll meet you later." He said and hung the phone up.

I didn't even have the patience to call him back, because Shafee came out to tell me the doctor was out. I walked in and noticed, whom I'm assuming her mother is, roll her eyes.

"Are you the family of Miss. Buffalo or Mr. Sweet."

"Mr. Sweet?" I questioned and Misfit looked at me. The only Sweet, I know, is B-Huff.

"Yea, he was brought in, shortly after Miss Buffalo." I took my phone out my pocket and was about to send my sister a text.

"Do not text her to come up here." Misfit said, standing on front of me."

29

"WHAT?" I yelled but not too loud. He ran his hand over his face.

"There's a hit on your sister."

"Come again." He pushed me to the side.

"The hit was put on his baby mother, which none of us knew, at the time, who she was. The only one who can remove the hit, is K, I mean, Unique."

"Yo, this shit is fucking crazy."

"I know." We both stood there in our own thoughts.

"Look, let's see what the doctor's talking about and go from there." He went to walk away and I stopped him.

"Did you know who she was before sleeping with her?"

"No. I found out fifteen minutes before Unique was shot." He walked away and left me standing there. I went over to find out what the doctor was saying.

"Miss Buffalo, suffered two gunshot wounds. One... was to her hip and the second... was to her neck." I said the words in my head at the exact time, he did. I was only able to do it, because it's the exact spot, I hit my target.

"And the baby?" I questioned and everyone looked at me.

"I'm sorry but the trauma to her body, caused a miscarriage." I backed up and noticed everyone staring at me. The words in my mouth wouldn't come out. Hearing him, basically tell me; I'm the reason our child is dead, well Javier is, but I'm the one who executed the hit, had me at a loss for words.

I stormed outta the hospital so quick, if anyone called me, I couldn't hear them. I hopped in my car and drove straight to my sister's house. All I could think of, was Unique saying, she didn't wanna have more kids because of the other miscarriages and now look? Not only did I give her life, I took it away. A nigga was fucked up.

I pulled up to my sisters, jumped out the car and went to the door. She opened it and appeared to be disheveled herself. Did she know about Unique already?

"What's wrong?" She asked. I took a seat in the living room and laid my head back. I felt the few tears sliding down the side of my face.

"Unique lost the baby." She covered her mouth and sat next to me.

"How?"

"Krista, don't get mad." She looked at me with a crazy look.

See, my sister knew exactly the type of work, Mike and I used to do. Her and my mom hated it because the job, would take us away from them, for long periods of time and they always complained. Granted, the money was good and it's the reason we live good now. However, we left the life alone years ago, to live our life without spending time away from them.

Now, we go and do an order for Javier and unbeknownst to us, my damn woman is lying in a hospital bed and my child is in heaven. I know, we hit all types of people but I have to know if Javier was aware, Unique, K or whoever they call her, was my woman? Did he send me on the hit, purposely? Why is he even worried about the organization she's running? I don't understand none of this.

"If you're telling me not to get mad, it has to be bad." She folded her arms across her chest and waited for me to speak.

I explained everything about the hit and she had tears coming down her face, for B-Huff and the baby, I lost. I hadn't even told her about Unique, having a hit out on her. It was crazy how one minute, we were living perfect and the next, we're stuck in so much chaos, we didn't even know half of why the shit was even done.

"Uncle Z." I heard my nephew say my name and jumped up.

"FUCK! Does Misfit know where you live?"

"Yea, why?"

"SHIT!" I snatched my nephew up and told her to pack a small bag. She didn't ask any questions and did what I said.

33

Once she finished, we walked out the house and to my car. I put my nephew in and told her, she had to leave. I started driving and stopped by a Walgreens and picked up two prepaid phones. Of course, she questioned why I did it and I promised to explain later. I tossed her phone in the trash and drove off. I didn't know where to go and it seemed like we were just driving. Krista, finally told me to drive somewhere that was an hour away. She had me stop at the food store first, to grab some things for her and my nephew. I only did it because we were away from town. When we got there, I noticed a small ranch house.

"Whose house is this?" I picked my nephew up, who fell asleep on the way.

"Gianna and I, stay here once in a while." I looked at her.

"It's a place we go for emergencies or when we want to get away and before you ask, no, he has no clue it exists."

"Good. Look, you have to stay here for a while."

"Why? What is really going on?" I sat her down

"There was a hit placed on B-Huff's baby mama." She jumped off the couch.

"Oh my God! Do they know who I am?" She started pacing the floor.

"They do now." I put my head down.

"Zander, what am I gonna do?"

"Right now, you're gonna stay here."

"But."

"He loves you sis. I may not care for him but he's the one, who told me not to let you come up there. If he was gonna allow anything to happen to you, he wouldn't have mentioned it." She shook her head. I headed to the door.

"Don't open this door for anyone, except me, Mike or Gianna." I turned around to look at her.

"And Krista."

"Yea." She wiped her eyes.

"DO NOT CALL OR TELL HIM WHERE YOU ARE." She said ok but I had to make her see why.

"Sis, he may have told me, not to let you come up there, but it doesn't mean you're out the clear. It could be a plot, to keep others from killing you, because he's the one who's supposed to do it."

"Zander, I.-"

"I know you love him and I'm sure, he feels the same. However, when you work with ruthless people, love takes a backseat and things still have to be done."

"Ok."

"I'll come get you when I find out more. Right now, tempers are high and they're most likely, trying hard to find you."

"Zander, go get Mike and Gianna. Bring them here and we can be safe together."

"Gianna is missing, which is why, I'm leaving. Our brother needs us and as much as I need a moment to myself, I don't have the time. I'll call you later." I kissed her forehead and waited to hear her put the deadbolt on. I prayed she took heed to my warning, about not calling him. If he does anything to my sister, I don't care who he is; I will fucking kill him.

Mike

"The fuck you mean, she disappeared?" I was pissed, hearing they couldn't locate Gianna.

I left her at seven this morning, did my job, returned by ten thirty and here it is hours later, and they still have no idea where she is. When I went to the security desk, of course their cameras weren't facing the angle of her room, so you couldn't see shit. Everyone who went in the direction of the room, came back towards the camera. Which leads me to believe, whoever did it, came from the back stairwell. But how they get down there with her? She had tons of therapy session and said there was some feeling in her leg. However, not enough to walk on her own.

"I went to get a wheelchair for her to go down to therapy, and she was gone by the time, I returned." The scared nurse said.

"Do you even hear how stupid that sounds? My girl, can't even walk. How the fuck did she get outta here?" My phone rang and it was Gianna's mom.

"Hello."

"Can you get here?"

"Mrs. Clayton, I was just about to call you. Something happened to.-" She cut me off and told me to meet her, at my house.

On my way out, I ran into my brother, who looked like shit. He started telling me the shit with Misfit, and how Unique lost his baby. I felt bad for him and wanted to dwell more on the story but right now, I had to get home. Something about the way Gianna's mom asked me to get there, didn't feel right. And why am I going to my house and not hers?

I thought about the way my girl looked at me this morning before I left. She kept asking if everything were ok and no matter how many times, I said yes, she knew something was off. The crazy part is, everything was good with me, but not with her. I shouldn't be leaving the hospital but what good is it gonna do, if they have no idea where she is. I definitely won't get the cops involved because they'll start asking too many questions.

I got out the car in front of my house and noticed Gianna's dad standing there smoking a cigarette. Now, being around her for these last few years and them, I've learned he only smokes, when he's pissed. The closer I got, the more aggravation, I could see on his face. Zander came behind me and we all stood there, smoking in silence. Hell yea, we sparked up a blunt. After we all finished, I opened the door and saw my girl sitting on the couch, crying. I ran over to her and checked to make sure she was good. She placed her hands on my face.

"I'm ok baby." I felt her lips touch mine. Her mom cleared her throat because neither of us wanted to let go.

"How'd you get here? What happened?"

"Baby, my parents brought me here." I turned to look at them and they sat down. I knew, it was more to the story and braced myself for the bullshit.

"Why?"

"Mike, after you left this morning, I was waiting for the girl to take me to therapy." I nodded as she continued.

"My phone rang and it was a photo of Andre." I gave her a side eye.

"EXACTLY! I wanted to know why the hell someone was sending me, of all people, a photo of him. Anyway, another text came through and it said, *Mike, won't always be there to save you. And you can't run, especially, now that you're crippled.*" I was pissed someone threw in there, the disability she was currently facing.

"I didn't pay it any mind, until the last message came across." She started crying again, which only made me angrier.

"What did it say?" She showed me the message.

You better tell Mike, if he doesn't comply with the list, I'm sending him, you're dead. Oh wait! And the outfit you're wearing, accentuates all your curves. The person sent a smiley face to her.

"The only person this could be, is Javier." I handed the phone to Zander.

"How did you get her out?" I asked her dad.

"I came up the back steps and got her." I turned back to Gia.

"Why didn't you call me?"

"Mike, you said, you'd be busy and I didn't wanna bother you. I would've called you sooner but I wasn't sure what time, you'd finish. I took a chance on my mom calling you."

"Don't ever do that shit to me again. I thought someone took you from the hospital." I kissed her forehead and sat next to her.

For the next hour or so, Zander and I, explained as much as we could about our job, without mentioning everything. You could tell he wanted to go see Unique at the hospital, but his regret wouldn't allow him. He blames himself for killing his baby and her ending up in the hospital.

We usually don't do blind missions, the way we did this one; however, we had no idea, Unique was deep in the game. Shit, the way Zander explained it, she was the fucking boss and anything she said goes, which is why the hit on Krista, is still active. Thank goodness, she was safe, for the moment. We wouldn't have no it was her anyway because the hoodie had her face covered.

After they all left, I ordered some food and carried Gia upstairs, to take a bath. Like I said before, she can barely walk but she does try to stand on her own. The bath isn't too low and she wanted me to get in with her. I told her another time, took a shower on the other side and waited for the food to come. While, I sat there watching her relax in the tub, I got on my laptop and did some searching of my own. I'm assuming its

Javier, that threatened my girl, however, the text didn't come from his number and Zander, nor I, received a list.

I went to a site and input the phone number. Yes, I can hack into anything; including FBI, CIA and any other federal files. Of course, the person who called had a pre-paid device and there's no way to track it. I started looking for where the phone was purchased. I was so deep into looking, Gia had to yell at me to get the door. Evidently, the food came and I ignored her twice.

I put the laptop on my bed and ran down the steps. I swear, this house is nice as hell and worth the money. Unfortunately, it's too damn big for me. I would rather everything be on the same floor. All these damn steps and then, the amount of space in each room, is ridiculous, if you ask me. But, it's what my girl wanted.

I opened the door and paid the delivery driver. I also, noticed a pair of headlights at the end of my driveway. It didn't make me nervous one bit and closed the door. I put the food in the kitchen, opened my back door, jumped the fence and ran down the grass. Our neighbor lived a mile up the road, so it was open land. When I reached the car, the person had their head down. I pulled my gun out and snatched the door. My eyes damn near bucked out my head, when I saw who it was.

"Hello Mike." She said and got out the car. Here was this bitch, front and center and I wanted to kill her, for shooting Gia; however, after seeing her stomach, I couldn't do it.

"What the fuck are you doing here?"

"I followed you from the hospital." I sucked my teeth. I was slacking by not checking my surroundings.

"I should kill you, right now." She smirked.

"But you won't because our son, is keeping you from doing it."

"Son?" I found myself reaching to touch her stomach and pulled away. She grabbed my hand and placed it on her belly.

"You can touch him." I moved my hand.

"You have to go." I pushed her back in the car.

45

"Mike, I don't have anywhere to go. I tried to contact Unique, but they said she was shot. You know, I don't have anyone else." I stared to try and see, if she were lying. Unfortunately, I couldn't tell. I reached in my pocket and passed her my black card.

"Get a room and text me, where you're staying. I'll be there to get my card tomorrow." She stood on her tippy toes and kissed my cheek. I watched her pull off and ran back to the house. I closed the door and heard Gia calling me from upstairs. I took off running because a nigga forgot, she was in the tub. She had tears rolling down her face and I felt like shit. How I leave her, to entertain the same bitch, who tried to take her away from me?

"I'm sorry baby."

"Where were you? I was calling you. Mike, I thought something happened when you answered the door." I wiped her eyes and started washing her up. The water was a little cold, so I turned on the hot and finished.

"Mike, where were you?" She asked after putting her clothes on.

"There was someone at the gate but they left before I got there." I spit the lie out perfectly. Never in my life, have I lied to Gia and I didn't want to. However, I know she wanted to kill Ashanti; pregnant or not and right now, I'm not sure if its my kid. Therefore; until we know for sure, I'm gonna keep them away from each other.

Gianna

Mike thinks I'm stupid and I'm gonna let him. See, when the door rang, he disappeared. Who leaves their disabled women in the tub, to go check on a suspicious car? He had every right to check it out, but he should've told me and made sure I was at least, out the tub. Anything, could've happened to him and I would've never known. If that's not bad, his phone went off while we were eating and it was next to me. He didn't hear it because he ran in the kitchen to grab me some more soda. I picked it up to look, like always because we never hid anything on our phones and it was locked.

He came in the room, handed me my soda and sat back down. I know something was off and whatever it is, I hope, he's ready for the consequences to his actions. I'm not about to deal with another cheater or a man, who's keeping secrets. If he has someone else or even wanna be with another woman, he needs to let me go. I hate for a man to keep a chick around until he's ready to stop playing. Andre did the same thing and then apologized, when he realized, my ass was gone for good. They say you never miss your water, until the well runs dry,

I waited for him put the food up and said I was ready to go upstairs. I hated he had to carry me everywhere. He claimed not to mind, but I did. We get so used to being able to do everything, that the minute we can't, shit feels off. Like now, he's undressing and my ass is turned on. I wanna have sex with him but will I feel anything? Should I even waste my time, trying?

"Come here Mike." He walked over to the bed and stood in front of me. It's been a few weeks, since the shooting and I know he's horny.

"Yea." He stood in front of me. I moved my legs over, to hang off the bed and stared up at him. I loved the hell outta Mike and would be hurt, if he cheated. The love I felt for him, is much stronger than the love, I shared with Andre. It could be because we flirted so much and never been intimate. Now, that I've had him, I don't want anyone else to.

"You know, I love you right?" He lifted my chin up.

"What's wrong?" I stuck my hand in his shorts to distract him from the question, he asked. I didn't wanna answer.

"Shit, it feels good." He moaned a little, when I put my mouth on the tip.

"How good?"

"Realllll gooddddd. Shit." I juggled his balls in my hand and sucked, like my life depended on it. He needed to know, no other woman is gonna do him, the way his woman will.

"Fuck this." He pushed me back, lifted my legs and placed them on his shoulder. I felt a twinge in my legs but never mentioned it. The doctor said my body would react at different times. What he didn't tell me, was I'd feel this big ass African dick.

"Ahhhhh." I screamed out.

"Yea ma. You missed your man's dick. Look how much she's cumming already." He wasn't lying. A few seconds after he entered, my body reacted and juices shot out.

"Shit, I'm cumming." He laid on top of me.

"I love you Gia." He lifted his head and began kissing me. I could feel his dick twitching inside me.

"I love you too." He flipped me over, rested my stomach on the bed and held me up, as he entered from the back.

"Mike."

"Yea baby."

"Fuck, I'm cumming again." I gave him more of my body fluids and he went crazy. He held me up against the wall and fucked me so good, I thought the feeling in my legs came back.

"My sperm is about to fertilize some eggs." I laughed a little, until he dug deeper. My nails were in his shoulders and he was staring into my eyes.

"I love you so fucking much Gianna. Don't ever leave me."

"Mike." I tried to answer.

The orgasm was so strong between the both of us, he fell back on the bed, with me on top of him. Again, my legs felt weird but each time, I tried to get up, I couldn't. I laid on his chest and stared at him. His arm was over his eyes and he was trying to get his breathing under wrap.

"If you ever cheat, lie or keep any secrets from me, I will leave and never come back." He lifted himself on his elbows and stared at me. I used my arm, to push myself off him and laid on the bed. He sat up and wouldn't take his eyes off me. Whatever he was thinking, had him nervous. I could tell by the way he ran his hand over his face.

"Gia." I put my hand up for him to stop speaking. I needed him to hear me and understand.

"You came in my life and made me fall so deep in love with you, I can't even fathom, you disrespecting what we built.

However, I have to love myself more and if you can't keep it real with me or tell me things, we aren't gonna work. Mike, I love the ground you walk on, but I'll use that same ground, to walk away." He stood up and went in the bathroom. I heard him come out and felt him move the covers off, to wash me up. A few minutes later, he came and got in the bed with me and snuggled up behind me.

"I'm not letting you leave me, so stop saying it." He kissed the back of my neck. I pulled the covers over my body and wiped the tears from my eyes. I know in my heart, something isn't right and the longer he takes to tell me, the easier it's gonna be for me to leave.

****

The next day, he got up, helped me get ready for the day and carried me to the car. I didn't know where we were going and he wouldn't say. It took us a while but he pulled up at some jewelry store. I looked at him crazy because I know he wasn't doing, what I think he was. He always said, I had to tell him yes first and then he'll buy a ring. However, here we are in front of Tiffany's. He took that stupid wheelchair out and helped me in it. Looking at me, one would think, I may have a broken foot or something because I looked normal. My clothes were on point, my hair was done and he made me wear Jordan's for some reason. But the truth is, my bottom half, still has yet to work properly.

"Good morning, Mr. Brown. We have it ready for you." He put the brakes on my chair and sat next to me. I notice his phone ringing and once he looked at it, he hit ignore. Now, my radar already being up, knew it was someone he had no business talking to.

"Hi, Miss Clayton. My name is Morris." The man extended his hand for me to shake.

"Mike, what are we doing here?" Just as I asked the question, Morris opened a black velvet box and my mouth hit the floor.

"I see you like this one." He smiled and told me to hold my hand out.

"This is a 10-karat ring, in a solitaire cushion shape, rose gold, cut diamond."

"How much does this ring costs?" He looked at Mike, who nodded for him to tell me.

"Ma'am, this ring costs approximately, 1.5 million dollars." Just as he slid it on, I moved my hand away. The shit was beyond expensive and a five-thousand-dollar ring would've been fine for me. Mike signaled for the guy to hand him the ring. I tried to tell him, it was too much but he wasn't trying to hear it.

"Gianna Clayton, you are the woman, I've been waiting for all my life. This ring may be expensive in your eyes, but no amount of money, could top what you're worth to me. It took us a long time to find our way to each other and now that we have, I don't wanna waste any more time, making you my wife. I know, I said you had to say yes before I brought the ring, but I also know, you love me, as much as I love you and want the same thing." He pushed his chair out and got on one knee.

"Will you marry me?"

"Yes baby. Yes." I was shaking so bad, he had to hold my hand, to slide the ring on. He lifted me out the chair and wrapped my legs on his waist.

"This doesn't define anything." He smacked my legs.

"You will walk again and I promise not to cheat, or lie to you." I noticed he kept secrets outta it. Maybe the text or call was him and this guy setting things up for today. I'm still gonna keep it in the back of my head though. My gut is never wrong.

He helped me in the car and we drove back, holding hands. I asked if he could take me to see Krista and lil man. I wasn't allowed to call her and I'm sure she was lonely as hell out there. Yea, there was cable in the house, and a playground in the back but it does get boring out here.

A week at the most is how long, I stay and then I need to get to my life. She's been here for longer than that, so I can only imagine, how bored she is. When we pulled up, Zander's car was there. At least, we'll all be under one roof again.

Zander

Mike and Gianna showed up at the house, Krista was staying at, and while Krista and Gianna, gushed over the engagement ring and how he proposed, I saw the look of stress on his face. I congratulated them and asked him to come outside to have a drink and smoke with me. I'm sure, whatever he's about to tell me, we both would need it. I had lil man follow us outside and he ran straight to the sliding board. Gia and Krista had this house set up nice and made sure it was kid friendly.

"What up?" He let his head fall back on the seat and blew smoke out his breath.

"Ashanti is back." I almost choked on the drink. I knew what was coming next without him saying it. He was having an issue with killing her because she was pregnant and I understood. I'm not sure, I could kill my kids mother either.

"Where she at now?"

"Bro. I gave her my card to get a hotel room. She claims the only person who would help her is Unique and she's outta commission. I got an alert on my phone, from the credit card company. Do you know this bitch went to the damn Waldorf Astoria in New York, which in my opinion, is too fucking much?" I nodded.

"That's not the best part."

"What she do?"

"Man, this bitch went shopping on 5th avenue today and brought twenty-five thousand dollars' worth of shit." He had to pat me on the back, so I would stop coughing.

"Yo, go get your shit."

"Nah. I cut the card off. Gianna said some things to me last night and a nigga was shook."

"What she say?" He started telling me how Gia planned on leaving him, if he held any secrets, cheats or lies to her. She doesn't want him to do the same thing, Andre did. It's understandable and I told Mike to tell her.

"She wants Ashanti dead for almost killing her, and Z, you know I do too. I can't take the chance of this being my kid and.-"

"Say no more." Mike and I, are real big on family, even though we didn't have a huge one. It didn't stop us from spoiling the hell outta our sister and nephew. Both of them, received any and everything they wanted and now so did Gianna.

"I have to tell her." I could see how it was eating him up but he knew what had to be done; regardless of what the outcome would be. Mike, isn't used to being a one-woman man and Gianna, is the only woman, who is able to make him change into one. The crazy part is, he's in love with her and doesn't want anyone else. Unfortunately, now that Ashanti is back, she's gonna make it real hard and it's in his best interest to tell Gianna, before she does.

"Zander and Mike, can you bring Brian in for dinner." Krista yelled out. She was cooking before they got here. We did like she asked and Mike closed and locked the back door.

We all stayed up half the night talking and watching movies. It got so late, Mike and Gianna stayed in the other room.

****

Once everyone was asleep, I locked up and drove to the hospital, like I've done every night. Unique, would be so high on pain medication, she wouldn't know I was here and I'd stay all night, watching her sleep. Her father came by in the morning once and caught me asleep in the chair. He never asked who I was and neither did the security, who stood outside her door. I assumed Misfit gave them permission to let me in.

If you're wondering why I come at night, its because I couldn't face her awake. I'm the reason she's in here and why our child is gone. I'm not the type of dude to keep secrets from my woman and I know, if she asks what happened, I'll tell her. The look on her face will probably kill me. It's better for me to deal with it alone right now.

"Where is she?" I heard as I walked in her room. I was shocked to see him here, but then again, she is his daughters mother.

"You must be crazy, if you think, I'd tell you where she is." He stood up and came my way.

"What you fail to realize is, I found out who she was before this happened. I was twenty feet away from her, as she argued with that fuck nigga and could've pulled the trigger. Trust me bro. If I wanted her dead, she would be." He bumped my shoulder and walked out. I could tell he was hurting for my sister, but I couldn't chance it either.

"I'll have her call you." He stopped and turned around.

"I need to see, she's ok." I pulled my phone out and showed him a photo of her and my nephew. The date on the phone was time stamped from earlier. I had taken it when she was coloring a picture with him. He ran his hand across my phone and smiled.

"I'm glad she's ok. I wanna talk to her but keep her where she is." I put my phone up and stared at him. It's like he wanted to say more and couldn't.

"She misses you too." I saw the grin on his face.

"Keep her there, until I tell you she's safe. Right now, motherfuckers are looking for her and like I told you before, the only person who can call the hit off, doesn't even know yet. Your best bet, is to wait for her to see you and let her know what's going on. She loves you Zander and wants to know, why you're not here when she's awake. Tell her the truth about what happened, otherwise, its gonna hurt more, if she hears it from me."

"What?" He came closer to me.

"I know you work for Javier and the one who did this." I fell against the wall.

"I could kill you right now, but I know, you had no idea who she was, which, I blame her for. Sadly, both of you keeping secrets caused you to lose a child. I know that shit hurts because Krista never told me, when she lost the one, we were gonna have." He said and walked off with his head down. How the hell did he know? Did Javier tell him and what does he mean, the one him and Krista lost? She never mentioned losing a kid.

I got myself together and went in the room, only to find Unique, wide awake. She smiled and it caused me to smile. As bad as, I wanted to go off on her about who she is, I couldn't. She patted the bed for me to sit next to her. I took my shoes off and climbed in with her. I loved this woman and wanted nothing to do, then protect her. How can I though, when she kept her true identity a secret?

"I'm sorry." We both said at the same time.

"You didn't know Zander and I should've told you exactly who I was. I blame myself." She put her head down.

"Wait! How did you know, I did it?"

"Misfit told me, he had to reveal my identity to you." I nodded.

"Therefore, you should know, finding out who was behind the hit, wouldn't be hard. Granted, I cried after they told me, you were the one who did it. It wasn't until my father mentioned, who the person was working with Javier, that told us, you and Mike, only received a letter and description of who the targets would be. I should've told you sooner because you would've automatically known, it was me at the meeting." I wiped her eyes.

"Unique, I'm pissed and feel like he set me up to do this."

"What do you mean?"

"Javier, knows Mike and I, never go in a situation blind. However, he assured us nothing would go wrong and the people aren't to be killed. We thought it was weird because he never left his victims alive. Instead of questioning him further, we just went with it. The day it happened, we did what he asked and bounced outta the hotel. Both of us, were trying to get back, to you and Gianna. You wanted to talk and I felt it was something important, since it was the third time you brought it up. Anyway, once I found out it was you, I called him up and he refused to discuss it over the phone and now, it's like he fell off the grid. His number is no longer in service and B-Huff is missing."

"Someone had him removed right after the doctor told my family, he was there."

"What?"

"Yea. He was a dead man."

"How are you though? Can you have more kids?" She laid her head back.

"I can but right now, I don't wanna think about it." I kissed her on the lips and told her, I understood. This is her third miscarriage and probably taking a toll on her right now.

"I love you Unique and I'm sorry for hurting you and making us lose a child."

"I love you too and when its meant to happen, it will. Ain't that what you said?"

"It sure is and the minute you're ready, I'll give you another one." She pulled me in for a kiss and the two of us fell asleep, not too long after. I still had to speak to her about Krista but it'll have to wait until tomorrow. I hadn't slept well since she's been here, and now that I know she's good, I plan on sleeping well, with her right by my side.

Unique

"You have to kill him." My father said after I woke up from the shooting. Now, with me just opening my eyes, I had no idea who he was speaking of.

"Once she wakes up, we'll let her decide." I heard my brother say, which only pissed my father off.

"I'm woke." They both ran over to me.

"What happened?"

"Misfit said, you were standing there and someone shot you." My hands immediately went to my stomach. Both of them putting their heads down, confirmed what I knew, once he mentioned the shooting. I had lost another child. I wanted to cry but there will be other times for that.

"Where's Angel?" They told me home with my mom. I glanced around the room the best I could with this big ass patch on my neck.

"Don't look for that sucker." My father had a lot of venom in his voice.

"Unique, do you know who Zander really is?"

"He works for the cable company." My father shook his head.

"He does, however he works for Javier and the one who did this." Shafee pointed to my stomach. I was pissed because Ronald gave me a ton of information on him, so how did he miss this?

"No, he wouldn't risk losing our baby." Now, I felt the tears streaming down my face.

"He has to die Unique." My father was still shouting the same shit out.

"Sis, he didn't know who you were. Why didn't you tell him?" I should've told him sooner. Shafee, appeared to feel bad, however, my dad was ranting the entire time.

"We weren't together long enough and I wasn't sure if I could trust him. The day, I finally got up the courage to tell

him, this happened. Oh my God, is anyone else hurt? Misfit,

Champ, where are they?"

"They're fine. You know Misfit has been here and

won't allow anyone in, unless he says its ok. B-Huff was shot

too, but he's in the wind. Someone took him outta here, before

we could get to him."

"Get some rest sis. I'll see you soon." My brother

kissed my forehead and my dad did the same. Misfit came in

later that day and explained more to me and none of us, have

spoken about the incident since.

Over the next few days, everyone came to see me;

except Zander. When I asked Misfit about him, he sucked his

teeth but told me, he came at night. I guess after finding out,

I'm the one he shot, he probably doesn't wanna face me and I

don't blame him. How could I, when I'm just as much at fault,

as him?

I found out, I could still bare kids and that's what I was

hoping for. Unfortunately, I don't want any for a while. I have

to figure out why Javier wanted us hurt and not dead. I feel like

Zander. Who leaves their victims alive to retaliate? He was making a point but what was it? And why now, of all times? Whatever the reason, I'm gonna find out, even if I have to set Zander up to find out the truth. It's the least he can do, after killing our baby.

****

"Who lives here?" Zander questioned me, when he pulled up to my mansion. I totally forgot he had no idea about this place.

"Umm, I do." I said after he opened the door on my side.

"I thought you lived in a condo." He stood there pissed. His eyebrows were almost connecting and I could see his face becoming angrier.

"Zander, does it matter? I had more than one place." I walked slowly to the door and felt his presence behind me. I opened it and he slammed it.

"What the fuck you mean Unique?"

"I'm saying, I have two places."

"Why didn't you tell me about this house?" I may as well tell him the truth. I mean shit, he clearly knows who I am now. No need to keep lying.

"I purchased the condo, so I wouldn't embarrass you."

"Embarrass me?"

"Zander, I didn't know you had money." He chuckled. He never told me he did, but if he worked for Javier, I knew doing hits, paid hella good money.

"Let me get this right." He stood with his arms folded.

"You lie about where you live because you thought, I'd be in my feelings, for you having more money than me. You try and make a fool outta me and my sister and the dinner. Then, I almost kill you because you wouldn't reveal who the fuck you really were."

"Basically." I shrugged my shoulders and he slammed me against the wall, so hard, I thought my stitches would bust.

When Zander shot me, he got me in the neck but no major artery was hit. The one in my hip, shattered a few bones inside and has me walking with a limp. The doctor said it would take me some time and therapy, to walk normal again, but it's possible.

"We lost a fucking child, from you having secrets and all you say is basically."

"You had a secret too, Zander. I didn't know you were a shooter."

"Don't even try it Unique." He let me go and slammed his hand against the wall.

"You knew everything about me, and when you didn't, you had someone look into me."

"Who told you that?" I wondered because I never told anyone about Ron giving me information.

"No one. If you're a savage, Boss or whatever, it's your job to check the person out, which is how you found out my phone number and where I lived." I put my head down.

"I told you about a job I used to do, and regardless of what it was, you never even asked questions. If I had a clue of the shit you were into, I would've made sure you weren't the target. FUCK!" He yelled out and headed for the door.

"Is anything about what you felt for me, real?" I was shocked he'd asked me that. I walked up to him.

"Zander, I don't want anyone else and my feelings are definitely real. I'm sorry for keeping you in the dark about my job. I told you, I wasn't ready for kids and it happened anyway. I was excited and ready to bring a life in this world with you, but it wasn't our time. And how can you ask me if my feelings were real?"

"Because no woman would go through purchasing a showroom house, to keep her man from knowing, she had money. No woman, would try and come for her ex's new chick, to try and prove a point. No woman, would keep something as important, as being a boss, from her man. And no woman, would allow her man to believe she's something, other than what she is." He opened the door to leave.

"Don't leave Zander. I'm sorry about everything."

"Unique, you have a lot of growing up to do and I'm not the type of nigga, to raise a grown woman."

"WHAT?" I shouted. Who the fuck did he think he was speaking to?

73

"You heard me. You out here acting like a damn child, when you don't get your way. You may not be with your ex but you're still consulting with him about shit. What the fuck were we even together for, if you couldn't be real with me?" I put my hand up.

"I don't care he works with you, Chanelle can't even sit with me at Burger King, without you tryna kill her. I made a promise not to disrespect you, but that's all you've done to me and I'm over it. I am in love with you Unique, but love ain't about to have me out here looking stupid. Call me when you grow up." He walked to his car and turned around.

"Oh, and take the hit off my sister."

"What? I don't have a hit out on your sister." I was confused as hell.

"Maybe, you should speak with your roll dog, Misfit. Let him fill you on." He got in his car and sped off. I sent Misfit a text and asked him to come see me. Zander, got me fucked up if he thinks, I'm gonna allow him to leave me. I'm not gonna stalk him, but he's gonna see me a lot, whether he wants to or not.

****

It's been a few days since I came home from the hospital, and I hadn't seen anyone besides my daughter. Misfit, was supposed to stop by but I had yet, to see him. He's most likely, trying to find Javier like everyone else. It's like he fell off the face of the earth and if I'm correct, B-Huff is with him. I wonder how the two of them linked up and if his brother knows. Yea, he and I have been working together to get him but obviously, Javier was a step ahead.

"Hey bitch." Ashanti said coming in the house. Her stomach was pretty big and she was rocking some high-end apparel.

She's my cousin because her mom, is my father's sister but they don't have money like us. My dad is stingy as hell and always told her, if she wanted to live like us, she had to work. Instead, she told him to fuck himself and she'd never ask him for a dime, and to this day she hasn't. Unfortunately, Ashanti wanted to live like she was rich and always going after ballers.

The reason she went after Mike is because Andre put her up to it. He wanted Gianna away from Mike. The only

75

thing is, he pushed them together because he couldn't stop fucking other chicks; my cousin included.

"What are you doing here? You know Mike wants to kill you." She waved me off and went in my living room.

"Girl, I already saw him. How you think, I'm dressed like this?" She pointed at her attire. I wasn't gonna ask questions about his money. It's obvious, him and Zander, are on the same team, therefore; I can only imagine how much he really has stashed away.

"Say what?" I was shocked. I thought for sure, he'd kill her on sight.

"Yup. I pulled up at his house and he came out. He felt my stomach, gave me his black card and you know a bitch lived it up, for the moment." She told me he cut the card off, and she had nowhere to go, which is why she's here.

"Ok, so what's next?"

"Nothing. There's a party, I wanna go to. You down?" The smirk on her face, told me she was up to something.

"My hip is fucked up and.-"

"Unique please. Security will be tight and no one will bother you anyway."

"Fine. Let me know when it is and we can go from there. Meanwhile, if he took the card away, where you staying?"

"Duh. At my own house. I left the day, his girl got shot, but now that I know he isn't as mad anymore, I took my ass right back."

"Ashanti, I love you to death but you're playing with fire. If his girl finds out you're in town, shit is gonna hit the fan."

"Mike, isn't going to let her touch me. I'm pregnant with his baby, remember?" She smirked and I shook my head.

Ashanti, never did listen to shit people said. Things always had to be done her way, and I guess she'll learn eventually, that niggas go to war for their women. Pregnant or not, Zander told me, Mike can't wait for her to deliver. I'm sure once she does, and if the baby ain't his, she's gonna die. She may be my cousin and I can protect her, but she's a wanna be side chick and I can't stand women like that. Whether, I know this Gianna chick or not, I know how it feels to be

cheated on.

Ashanti

Say what y'all want about me but a bitch don't give a fuck. Mike was my man first and best believe, a bitch got pregnant on purpose. Now, who the father is; right now, the jury is out.

See, Mike and I, met almost a year ago and we didn't hook up right away. He was always working, and so was I. However, he was way busier than me. Anyway, we ended up going out and slept together. No, it wasn't too soon because like I said, we were well acquainted already and meeting up, was the last thing to do. Long story short, he fucked the hell outta me and all I wanted to do, was keep him to myself. Low and behold, this Gianna bitch was in the way.

The day I met her, she was in the kitchen and at first, I thought she'd be nice but once her and Mike, joked around and he made a remark about, waiting on the right woman; I knew they had feelings for one another. Which is why, I made it my business to keep him entertained at my house. He only went home to change clothes, go to work and then come back. I started loving everything about him and made a vow, that no other woman would have him.

One night, we had a big fight over me accusing him of sleeping with Gianna. He left and I went to the store to grab ice cream and sulk all night. I ran into this guy named Andre, who I later found out, was in his feelings over some chick named Gianna. Well, let me tell you, we had sex a few times and a bitch was hooked on him, too. Mike, wasn't fucking with me like that, so why not?

Once we started talking and texting more, he invited me to his house. Gianna wasn't there and Andre, set up this entire candlelight dinner for me. I mean, rose petals and everything. Before we ate, he ran a bath, where the two of us, ended up having sex.

After we finished, he told me Gianna came home and saw us. I was petrified because what if she told Mike? He assured me, that my back was the only thing visible and she didn't come all the way in. I asked how he knew, this idiot said, he winked at her while I was riding him. This nigga was bold as hell. Here I am thinking we're being discreet and he's promoting the affair.

Over the next few weeks, he and I were sleeping together a lot, where Mike never touched me again. Now that I think about it, ever since the night she came and saw us, he never spoke, unless it was about the baby. I really tried to get Mike in bed but he was loyal as fuck to his girl, where Andre, gave zero fucks and fucked me all in their crib.

Now, I'm sitting in my house waiting on Mike to come see me. He said we needed to talk, but didn't mention what it was about. I heard a car pull up and opened the door. He stepped out and I wanted him to take me upstairs and give my pussy a beating, for being naughty.

"What's up?" He stood at the door, even after inviting him in.

"I'm a let you get away with spending my money."

"It was for the baby."

"Oh, the expensive hotel, is for the baby? Or these red bottoms, you're wearing? How about these diamond studs in your ears?"

"Who cares? You got it." He grinned.

"Exactly! I got it, which means, my girl has it and you're spending her money." I instantly got mad.

"Why are you here?"

"I came by to say, if you see my girl, go the other way. If you say, two words to her or even attempt to fight her, I'll forget you're pregnant and beat your face in." My mouth hit the floor.

"Oh, you thought the baby, would keep me from laying hands on you?"

"Mike."

"Mike, my ass. You kept this kid, to spite my girl. It's all good because even though, I won't lay hands on you right now, unless you touch my girl. I can't say what she'll do, if you two run into one another. Baby or not, she wants you dead." He turned around to leave.

"You'll let her kill me with our son?"

"I tried to ask her to wait but she isn't listening. Maybe her getting ready for our wedding, will keep her occupied." He hit me with the peace sign. I slammed my door and let out a scream. I hated Gianna and when the hell did he propose. It's obvious, I had to get her before she got me and I knew just the person to help me.

****

"Let me get this right. Gianna wants to kill you and the nigga proposed?" I nodded.

"She told me, they weren't a couple. I'm gonna kill her." Andre was angrier than I was.

The day at the gym, he went and apologized to her; only because his father made him. See, people don't know but Javier, is Andre's father. I know, crazy right. The two of them weren't speaking for years because of his relationship with Gianna. Javier, didn't like interracial dating. It's crazy though because Andre's mom, is black. He said it's different, since they both have dark complexions. *Go figure!*

Anyway, Javier had Mike and Zander, do a hit on some very important people, who turned out to be my cousin and B-Huff. I knew who the guy was because his name is big in the streets. I'm not sure why he placed a hit on him, but whatever. Andre, told me before, how his father was out the game for a

83

long time but wanted to get back in, since my uncle stepped down. I never understood, why people worked so hard to leave the game, only to try and get back in.

"Look. I think, this will work in our favor."

"What you mean?" He slammed the drink down and pulled me closer.

"If you can get her to meet you, we can get some pictures and send them to him. Mike, seems to be in love with her and pictures will definitely make him snap."

"Ok. First handle this." I stared down and his dick was at attention. Since, I was horny, he got exactly what he wanted, and so did I. After we finished, and cleaned ourselves up, he made the call. Surprisingly, she answered and agreed to meet up. Both of us headed out in different cars. I couldn't wait to see how this shit played out.

****

"Ashanti, don't say anything." He said and sat in the booth behind me. He sat opposite of where he wanted Gianna to sit, so she couldn't see me take any photos and I could hear the conversation.

84

It didn't take long for her to arrive, and when she did, I was shocked. I had no idea, she was in a wheelchair and why did she bring, the Krista bitch? Looking at her outfit, my ass instantly became jealous. Everything on her, appeared to be expensive, and the rock on her finger, couldn't be missed, either. Mike, was really taking care of her.

Krista, put the brake on her wheelchair and helped her slide in the seat. I could see them out the corner of my eye, so I don't know if Andre helped because my back was towards their booth.

"How are you Andre?" I heard her ask.

"What the fuck Gianna?" He snapped right away. I had to send him a text, to calm the fuck down, before he messes everything up, with his dumb ass.

"Andre, if you're gonna be hostile, I'm gonna leave."

"How the fuck you marrying a nigga, you claim never to have been interested in?"

"Andre, you know he and I were never intimate. However, you pushed me straight in his arms."

"Tha fuck you mean?" I could hear him getting angrier and glanced around the place to find Krista. I knew, it be a matter of time before he flipped and she asks to leave. I had to get some pictures fast. I noticed Krista outside on the phone and sent him a text to lean over and kiss Gianna.

When he text back, *ok*; I stood up and got my camera ready. I snapped a few of her sitting there, just in case, he couldn't get a good one. He stood up and went over to her side of the table. He grabbed her face quickly and slipped his tongue in her mouth. I caught his tongue come out, her hands on his face and her slapping the shit outta him. Of course, I'm not sending that one but the others, I am.

"Bitch, are you crazy?" I watched him bend her wrist back. I felt bad, because not only is she handicapped but he's about to snap it.

"Let go Andre. This is why we couldn't be together."

"Nah. We can't because you been fucking dude."

"I have not. He had someone and.-"

"Yes, you have."

"Andre, what happened to you apologizing for hurting me?" I laughed because it was a scam and she didn't even know.

"Shut the fuck up Gianna, or I swear, I'll break your nose."

"And, I'll shoot your fucking head off." I looked up and Krista was standing there with a gun, pointed at him. People in the restaurant started yelling and running out.

"You good Gia?" she nodded and I moved away. Gianna inched her way into the wheelchair, as Andre held his arms up.

"Andre, don't ever contact me again."

"This ain't over Gianna."

"Goodbye." She wheeled herself out the best she could. Her wrist was red and I'm sure in pain, but she kept it moving.

After they left, he asked if I got the pictures. I told him yes, and he said, its time to send them. I can't wait to see if they still get married. The crazy part is, I'm gonna wait until the right moment to send them. I need to see Mike's reaction to what his precious Gianna does when he's not around.

Krista

"You ok?" I asked Gia, as I helped her get in the car.

I had no business even coming to town, when my ass is wanted. However, Gia was with me, when Andre called and said he had something important to talk with her about. At first, she declined but then he said, Mike was in trouble. Not sure, why she assumed he was truthful but hey, this her shit.

"Yea. I don't know why, I thought he'd change."

"Girl bye. Once a woman beater, always one." She sucked her teeth.

"Don't get mad at me. Gia, the apology was nice, unfortunately, you can see he didn't really mean it. Why else would he try to snap your wrist, or threaten to break your nose? Whatever the reason for the apology, may be for something else."

"Like what?"

"Ugh, like you helping him find another place or giving him money." She waved her hand at me. I know she hated to go down memory lane, when it came to him but the truth is, what it is.

I drove to her house and Mike wasn't there, thank goodness. However, Gia, had an attitude. Zander, told me, Mike's not cheating and they've been working and trying to find Javier. He went missing and so did my son's father. Not that I'm missing him, but my son is and I'm sure, they'd both rip into me, if I even thought about asking where he was.

I opened the door and helped her inside. She asked me to stay while she took a bath. I did assist her in the tub fully dressed and when I walked out, somehow, she removed all her clothes and started the bath. After a half hour, she yelled for me. I handed her a towel through the shower curtain and then some clothes. See, Gianna was now able to stand and take small steps, as long as someone is on the side of her. She hadn't told Mike yet, which, I definitely didn't agree with. However, she'd tell him when she's ready.

I left her in the bed and locked up. They had a key made for me, in case Gia needed me and he could get here fast enough.

"You think he's cheating?" Gia asked when I answered the phone on my drive to the place, my son and I, have been staying at.

"No. He's not a cheater Gia and never has been. Zander told me they've been looking for Javier and it's taking up a lot of time." I saw headlights behind me and became nervous for some reason. Don't ask why, when the car dipped off down a different street. Paranoia was kicking my ass, that's for sure. My son wasn't even staying with me right now because of how scared I was. If these people wanted me, I'll be damned if he gets caught up.

"You're right. I'm going to bed."

"Alright. I'll text you when I get there."

"Ok." I hung up and pulled in front of the house an hour later.

The place was dark but I left the kitchen and porch light on. I grabbed the few bags of things, I brought from the store and stepped inside. Everything fell out my arms, when I saw him sitting on the couch staring at me. *How the fuck did he find me?*

"Why didn't you tell me who your son's father was?" I bent down to pick the things up and couldn't stop shaking.

"You… You never asked." I was stuttering and shit.

"Are you here to kill me?" He stood up and came towards me. I reached in my purse to find the gun, I just pulled on Andre, but he caught me.

"I'm gonna tell you the same thing, I told your brother." I nodded and let the tears fall down my face.

"If I wanted you dead, you would be." He put his face close to mine.

"And being you may be carrying my kid, you're not going anywhere, anytime soon." He picked the pregnancy test up off the floor. I purchased it at the store because its been a little over a month since we've seen each other and my period, is nowhere in sight.

"Misfit, I.-"

"Don't say a word until you take this test." He grabbed my hand and walked with me in the bathroom.

"Do you have to stand there?" He was about to speak but his phone rang, which caused him to step out.

At first, I sat on the toilet, with my head in my hands. No one knew, there was a possibility of me being pregnant. It was so many things going on and I didn't want to bother anyone with my issues. The chance of me carrying, is probably at a hundred percent.

After the miscarriage; only a few weeks went by and we had a lot of unprotected sex. In my office, at the house and once in the car. Not once, did we even consider me getting pregnant; well, I didn't anyway. Yes, it's always a chance but I was so busy letting him make up with me from the dinner, I paid it no mind.

I opened the test, stuck it in between my legs and filled it up with urine. I put some tissue on the sink and left it there. I started the shower, removed my clothes and stepped in. I stood inside thinking about, how much, I was in love with Misfit. This man had come into my life and swept me off my feet. I'm not complaining at all but finding out he's a killer, is making me rethink my choices of being with him.

I felt the wind seep in and turned around, to see him standing there naked, stroking himself, with a smile on his face.

93

I bit down on my lip because he had no idea, how much my body missed him.

"You won't lose this baby and I put my word on that." I nodded my head and moved closer to him and kneeled down. I never gave him a chance to protest or stop me.

"I missed you too Krista." He ran his hand through my hair, until he released all he had. I stood up and reached for a sponge to wash us up.

"Are you gonna kill me?" I felt him twist my body around. He placed both hands on my face and stared in my eyes.

"No and neither is anyone else." I didn't say anything.

"Do you trust me?" I shook my head yes.

"Then know, I will go to war with anyone who fucks with you; including Unique." I moved his hands and stepped back.

"Misfit, I don't want you to go against her for me. You two share a child and.-"

"My daughter will always be good; regardless, if we speak or not. You are gonna be the mother of my child, as well, and no one will come for you, without repercussions from me."

He placed soft kisses on my neck and let his fingers work

wonders in between my legs. The current was so strong, my

body shook like never before.

"Get up here." He said, lifting me in his arms and

sliding me down.

"Ahhhhh. Misfit, it's been a minute." I yelled and dug

my nails in his back.

"I think, you need to get used to him again, so it's

gonna be a long night."

"Ok." I whispered in his ear as hit my spot,

continuously. The two of us, literally went at it until after two

in the morning.

I was hungry and instead of getting up to cook, he

went to some fast food place and grabbed us some food. We

dogged it and passed out right after. I hope he meant what he

said about no one bothering me. My son was with my aunt and

I wanted him to come home, but not until, I knew for sure he

wouldn't be in any danger.

****

"I don't want you in town, unless you're with me or your brothers." I turned around and looked at him. I had gotten up to make us some brunch since it was after twelve.

"I'm tired of being here Misfit." He came behind me and put his face in my neck.

"I know you are. However, Unique hasn't called the hit off on you yet." I turned around.

"I'm not waiting for that to ever happen." He opened my robe and licked his lips.

"Maybe if your brother takes her back, she may." He put me on the counter.

"Do you know, that out of all the sex we had last night, your man never got to taste you."

"Misfit, you don't have toooooooooo." I screamed out. He had my body going crazy, from the way he was licking, sucking and biting down. My juices were coming down so fast, he had a hard time keeping up.

"I'm a need to feel inside, before I leave." He pulled me off the counter, turned me over and fucked me so good, I burned all the damn food. It didn't matter because he would end up buying me more.

"I'll see you later." He kissed my lips and stepped out the door. I watched him pull off and took my ass straight in the room and went back to sleep.

A few hours later, Zander came and woke me up. I could tell he was stressed out, especially since he showed me a text from Unique, saying she missed him. I'm not even sure why he broke up with her. I jumped in the shower and came out to find him falling asleep on the couch. He probably hasn't been sleeping either.

I went in the kitchen to make us something to eat and called my aunt. My son was talking my head off on the phone. He wanted me to come visit, which I am tomorrow. Thankfully, my cousin stays with my aunt and her kids are always there. I don't know what I would've done if I had to keep him here. With everything going on, I'm not sure if Brian will try to take him or what, so it's better this way.

"You think I should take her back?" Zander asked when I brought him a plate of food.

"Do you love her?"

"Yea." He started telling me the reason he left her. In my opinion, she was dumb as hell for renting or buying an extra condo, just so he wouldn't know how much money she had. I mean, who even thinks to do shit like that?

"Then go talk to her. Tell her you'll take her back but she needs to reveal everything to you. There can be no secrets and if you find out, she's lying, you'll leave her forever." He sat there eating but agreed, he'll do it eventually. He likes seeing her sweat. I wanted to smack him for saying that.

"So, you and Misfit, on good terms, huh?"

"Who told you that?" I put my head down.

"That hickey on your neck." I ran in the bathroom. He definitely left one.

"Whatever."

"Be careful sis. I would hate to kill him, if he pulls some dumb shit." He stood and walked it the kitchen to put his plate up.

"I'm pregnant." I let my head fall on the seat.

"At least, he won't kill you until you deliver." He started laughing like it was funny. I threw my fork at him.

"I'm just playing. Congratulations sis. He really loves you and I'm sure he won't allow anyone to bother you." I smiled because its exactly what Misfit said. At bad as our situation is, I believed he loved me.

"Alright, I'll see you later." He kissed my cheek and walked out. I picked up my phone to call my man.

"Hey baby. You good?" Misfit sounded so sexy on the phone.

"Yea, I wanted to tell you, I miss you."

"I miss your sexy ass too. I'll see you tonight though." As he spoke, there was a knock at the door.

My paranoia kicked in quickly. He must've heard the knocking because he started asking who was at the door. The crazy part is, I had no time to answer. He kicked the door open and stood over me like a raging bull. I dropped the phone on the couch and prayed Misfit heard everything going on.

Brian (B-Huff)

"How do you know where she is?" I asked Javier. He and I, were in the office of his house, discussing how we'd get Unique and her crew outta the picture.

Unique and I, met one day and exchanged phone numbers. We spoke often and even met up a few times for lunch but she'd never allow me to kiss, touch or even hug her. She claimed it was because I was with my son's mother. Who knows if she was telling the truth, but I gave her the benefit of the doubt. She was easy going, funny and I enjoyed talking to her. When Javier told me she was K, I became nervous because I gave her hella information. I'm hoping she doesn't ever tell him. Javier would most likely kill me, the second she said, I told her anything.

"I had someone follow her, when she left the restaurant with my son and her friend Gianna." I cringed listening to him say, people had eyes on her.

I never wanted anything to happen to Krista or my son, which is why, I went to her office to get her. I was very well aware, of the fate Javier had for Unique. Shit, he used me in the process, to make it look like he was after both of us. The purpose was to have me attend the meeting and hear whatever she was speaking about, however, he had me shot, before anything started. To make matters worse, he took me from the hospital and had me well taken care of; only to tell me, the Misfit dude, is in love with my baby mama. I asked, how he knew and he said, because she's still alive. Evidently, there was a hit on Krista but her brothers, along with him, kept her hidden pretty well.

This pissed me off even more, which is why, I'm standing here in front of her, as she shook like a leaf. Krista is the perfect woman for me, but I wanted my cake and eat it too. Unfortunately, she wasn't having it and left me. I can forgive her for leaving me but not for fucking around with the enemy. Don't get me wrong. She may not have been aware of the beef between us, but that day in the office, should have told her we didn't get along. Then to hear, he loves her, only fumes the fire I had inside.

"Where your nigga?" She backed away from me, but it wasn't fast enough. I snatched her by the hair and drug her over to the couch. Krista, must think. I forgot she carries a weapon. Shit, me and her brothers are the ones, who told her to do so. We can't always be around and at least, we would know, she'd be protected. The bad thing, is she never kept it close enough for reasons like this.

"Brian, why are you here?" I slammed her on the couch.

"What you mean, why am I here? You have my son. By the way, where is he?" I glanced around the house and didn't see any signs of him. No toys, or anything. My son always kept his shit lying everywhere.

"He's not here." She tried to get up and I pushed her back down.

"Brian, just leave."

"Nah. I want you to call your nigga and tell him, you're horny or something."

"Wait! You want me to set him up, to come and be ambushed by you?"

"That's what I said."

"Absolutely not. I wouldn't do it, if he asked me either. Brian, whatever the two of you have going on, please leave me out of it." I stared at her and realized this bitch wasn't saying no, to stay neutral. The bitch was in love with him too. Where the hell have I been all this time, not to see shit for what it really is? She told me at the park, but I was in such a hurry to get to the meeting, I nixed it off.

I heard the sound of vibration and looked around to see where it came from. I told her to move and when she refused, I backhanded her. I was getting tired of her saying no, to everything I asked.

"Who this?" I answered the phone. The number was unknown.

"IF YOU TOUCH ONE HAIR ON HER; I'M GONNA RIP YOUR HEAD OFF YOUR SHOULDERS." He shouted and I took the phone away from my ear.

"Too bad, you're not here to stop me. Damn, Krista, that pussy looking fat and juicy." I was fucking with him. She was dressed in jeans and a sweatshirt. A nigga, couldn't see a damn thing, if I wanted to.

"Stop it Brian." She smacked my hand away when I squeezed her tity. I looked at the phone and noticed he hung up.

"Ugh oh. I think your man, is pretty upset, I'm here."

"Just go."

"Oh, I'm leaving and you're coming with me."

"No, I'm not." I didn't give her a chance to get shoes on and grabbed her by the hair. I loved doing this shit. I swear, it gave you a good grip on the person and full control.

"Do you have her?" Javier asked, when I sat down in the driver's side. I had to put the child lock on the back door, so she couldn't get out. It didn't stop her from trying to kick the damn window out.

"Yea. Where you want me to meet you at?" Just as he was about to speak, two big trucks came speeding towards me. I looked behind and there were two more trucks. I would be a fool to think, they weren't for her but how the hell did he send someone so fast?

"Yo, I got company." I hung up and slowed down.

"Let me go Brian." I made her hop in the front seat. The doors to the truck opened and dudes stepped out with guns pointed.

"Get the fuck out bitch." When she opened the door, I lifted my leg and kicked her so hard in the back, she went flying out. I didn't even give her a chance to hit the ground before pulling off. I heard gunshots hitting my car and continued driving through it. I hit one of the trucks and soon felt, some of those bullets hit me. How in the hell did I get caught up in this shit with Javier? I need to sit my ass down and reevaluate, if being in charge is really worth all this.

****

"Where is she?" I heard Javier barking when I walked in his house. Not only did I end up in a shoot-out with some nigga, who loved Krista, but my ass, had two more bullets removed.

"He has her."

"What you mean he has her?"

"I mean, he had four SUV's block me in and I had no choice but to kick her out my car. If I knew it would be this much trouble trying to get her, I would have asked for a few of your men, to assist me." I leaned my head on the seat. I could hear him chuckle.

"This is what happens when you send a boy, to do a man's job."

"Fuck you!" I closed my eyes and not even two seconds later, I felt a few hard blows to my face. I opened my eyes and it was one of Javier's henchmen, standing over top of me.

"What the fuck?"

"B-Huff, don't come in my house, disrespecting me and then asking, what the fuck? I sent you to do the smallest thing, and you couldn't handle it. How do I know, you'll be able to handle an empire?" I spit blood out on his floor and immediately regretted it. The look on Javier's face said it all. I used the sleeve of my shirt to clean it up.

Javier isn't a man, who tolerates a lot, however, since we were supposed to be a team, I thought, he'd have my back.

I guess not, because the way he's staring at me, had me a little nervous. I didn't wanna die, but I'm not about to let him do whatever he wants to me either. Granted, I let him talk me into making an attempt to bring Krista back but he's going too far with letting his guys hit me.

"Call Unique." He said and I gave him a crazy look. Now we both know who she really is, and me calling her, will only make her trace the call and kill me, sooner than later.

"And say what?"

"Tell her you wanna meet. If she agrees, get a time and place and I'll handle everything from there, since you can't seem to do shit right." I sucked my teeth and made the call.

"How are you Brian?" She sang in the phone. It was like she's been waiting on my call.

"I'm good. How are you?"

"Never been better."

"Look, the meeting didn't go as planned and I wanted to know, if we could meet up and continue with the plans, the way we were supposed to."

"Sure. Time and place." Javier mouthed a destination, date and time for the meeting. Once I gave it to her, she hung up and he looked at me.

"At least, you did something right. Now, get the fuck out my house."

"WHAT!"

"Did I stutter?" I didn't even respond and stood to leave. I turned around to see him speaking to his guards. I thought working with Javier would benefit both of us but now I see, he's in this for his own personal reasons. Whatever they are, hopefully Unique, K or whatever she goes by, will bring him to his knees. I can see, he's gonna be a problem if he makes it out alive, from their meeting.

Misfit

"Shit!" I ran over to Krista, when I saw him push her out his truck. I knew it was B-Huff and as bad as I wanted him, it had to wait.

The moment someone began knocking on her door, I had already hopped in my truck. Of course, everyone with me, followed suit. It took me forty minutes to get there and when we did, I saw him pulling out the driveway. How the hell did he even know where she was?

"You ok?" I lifted her up and she grabbed on my neck, tightly.

"I need to go to the hospital." She didn't have to tell me because she was going regardless.

"Did he hurt you? Please don't tell me, he touched you." She shook her head no, as I sat her in the truck. I blew out a sigh of relief.

I pulled up at the hospital and helped her out. The doctors had a nurse take her upstairs to the labor and delivery floor. Evidently, if you're pregnant, you get seen up there and not in the ER. It's fine with me because once she got undressed and on the bed, they placed monitors on her belly and I heard my kids' heartbeat, for the first time. Come to find out, Krista was five weeks, which is when she surprised me with the freaky shit. Actually, it was right before, I found out who her baby father was.

The two of us sat there for two hours. The doctor did an internal check and I wasn't really feeling him, stick that thing in her pussy. The only thing entering her, should be my dick or even a tampon. I could tell she was uncomfortable with me standing there but I damn sure wasn't leaving. These GYN doctors already get a free feel, when they stick their fingers in women. He wouldn't get a chance to feel my girl up.

After he gave us discharge papers and an earful of her taking it easy, I drove her to my house. When we first pulled up, she wasn't happy at all. I had to basically make her get out and go in. Before I opened the door, she grabbed the back of my shirt and pulled me in for a kiss. I swear, she was making me fall harder and harder for her, and she wasn't even doing much. I guess after seeing the way, I treated Unique and not appreciating her, the little things Krista did, turned me on and made me more grateful to have her in my life.

I opened the door quietly, since it was late, locked it and led her in my bedroom.

"Baby, I don't have anything to wear." She whined and started undressing to get in the shower.

"You're sleeping naked anyway. Does it matter?" She started laughing and left me standing there. I sent a text message to Unique and told her, we needed to talk. I haven't heard a thing about the hit being lifted, which meant Zander, hasn't made up with her yet. I removed my clothes and joined Krista in the shower. I was about to have a long night with her.

****

"Daddy, who's in your room?" Angel asked when she came in the kitchen. My mom was up making breakfast for everyone; including Krista, who she seemed to love.

"What I tell you about being grown?"

"Daddy, I went to wake you up and the door was locked. You never lock the door."

"Angel, sit down and let me talk to you." My mom was shaking her head and scrambling the eggs.

"Daddy, has a new female friend, or should I say, girlfriend."

"But, I want you and mommy back together." Just as she said that, I felt a presence behind me and it was Krista. The look of sadness was on her face and I hated it. The fact Angel said that shit while she stood there, didn't sit right with me. It's like she did it on purpose.

"Umm. I'm just gonna leave."

"Krista, I made you breakfast." My mom said.

"Thank you so much Carrie, but I think Misfit has some things he needs to handle. I don't wanna intrude."

"You're not intruding." She pointed to Angel who had an evil look on her face. Her arms were folded and she stood up.

"My daddy may like you, but I don't, and you can't take him from me." I snapped my head to look at her.

"Angel, I'm not trying to take your daddy away from you." I could see Krista trying and gave her an A for effort but Angel wasn't trying to hear shit.

"If you have a baby by her, I'll hate it and pinch it all the time." Krista's mouth flew open and so did my mom's. I snatched Angel's ass up and took her in the living room. Say what you want, but I put her over my knee and beat her ass. I've never put my hands on her; except to pop her in the mouth but she was going overboard. Who the fuck did she think she was?

"I'm sorry daddy. Please don't hit me no more." I smacked her ass a few more times and sent her upstairs.

"Misfit." I put my hand up at Krista. I could see she was upset but Angel had to be taught a lesson.

"Sit down to eat." At first, she stood there. I had to pull the chair out and make her sit.

"It's about time you beat her ass. Lord knows, she needed it." My mom said and sat a plate in front of Krista.

After she ate, I drove her to her house and went in behind her. I still wasn't comfortable allowing her to go home.

113

Especially now, with her dumb ass baby daddy, doing pop ups. But if she's closer to me and her brothers, B-Huff, would think twice about tryna get at her.

"Misfit, I'm sorry you had to give her a butt whooping."

"Don't be Krista. She has gotten away with a lot of things and it was time."

"I understand."

"It's partly my fault for letting her get away with so much over the years. I mean, I won't even let her mother get in her ass."

"Misfit, maybe it's too much for her. She is so used to her parents being together, it's probably a lot going on in her head."

"And that's cool, but disrespect won't ever be tolerated. My daughter is my life but she also knows better and I think she was trying to push you away."

"Really!"

"Yes. It's no excuse for the disrespect but you're the first woman, she's seen around and tested her limits. I bet she won't test shit no more." Krista shook her head and went in the bathroom. My phone started ringing and it was Unique. I knew she would be calling eventually, because she was picking Angel up today. I'm sure she got an earful.

"What up?"

"It's about damn time you whooped her ass." She laughed in the phone.

"Whatever."

"Don't whatever me. That's what your ass gets. Always, letting her get away with shit and now look? She done pissed you off so bad, you had to dig in that ass." I didn't find shit funny but she sure as hell did. I get it though. I let Angel do and say mad shit, and never allowed anyone to discipline her.

"Is that what you called me for?" I was pissed she thought it was funny because even though, I whooped my daughter, I still felt bad. I'll never tell her that because she'll feed off that.

"That and to have a meeting. I've already told everyone to meet at a different location in about an hour. Can you make it? I know something kicked off with your girlfriend last night."

"Damn, how you know?"

"Really Misfit!" I had to chuckle myself. I look at her as Unique more than I do, as K and forget, she finds out everything.

"I'll be there." She hung up. I turned around to see Krista crying.

"What's wrong?" I jumped up and ran over to her.

"Are you trying to be with your baby mama?"

"WHAT?" I shouted.

"I heard you talking and aren't you about to meet up with her?" I sat her down.

"Krista, Unique and I, are connected by our daughter and work. Trust me, when I say, you are the only one I want. However, if she calls for work or about my daughter, I will take the call. I need you to understand, that you're a major part of my life now and if this is gonna work, any insecurities you have, need to be checked at the door." She nodded her head and claimed to get it, but did she? I don't have time to cater to

116

jealousy. Yes, I fucked up before but it wasn't with her and if she's gonna go off my past, we can end this now.

"Now, I'll be back later on and we can discuss whatever you want."

"Really! I want my son to come home."

"He will." I lifted her face and kissed her lips.

"Lock up." I walked out and waited to hear the dead bolt go on. I love Krista but I'm definitely not about to deal with no bullshit.

****

"As you all know, Javier is the person behind the hit." Unique said and everyone shook their head. Some were aware and others weren't.

"I want you all to take a good look at everyone in this room." They all started doing as she said.

"One person, in particular, worked alongside of Javier, which is how he was able to know where the meeting was, what I'd be wearing and a few other things going on in the organization." I saw K, take her gun from behind her waist. Me,

117

Shafee and Champ all did the same thing. K, didn't use her weapon unless someone really pissed her off.

"Isn't that right, Chico?" She didn't give him time to speak and shot him at point blank range, in the face.

"You see, I know and find out a lot more, than most of you know. For example, Pop, you've been stealing money and blaming poor Tito over there." She wasted no time, killing him either.

"And Rob, you were my accountant." I could see Rob sweating like a slave.

"You thought when I was shot, I wouldn't check my money. You thought it was ok to remove over a hundred thousand dollars outta my account."

"K, wait!" He pleaded.

"Wait for what?"

"It was for my mom. She was sick and.-"

"Your mom being sick, had nothing to do with me. And you could've asked me to help, instead of taking."

"I'm sorry." He put his head down.

"No need to be. You can join your mom, father and baby mom's in hell."

BOOM!

His brains were on the back wall, along with Tito and Chico. See, K didn't let anyone know how much of a savage she was, previously because it would've taken away from her loving Zander. I say that because, she really wanted him to know who she was, but scared he would leave her in the process. It's the exact reason, she never fully admitted to the shit with Chanelle. You must've been a fool to think, she wouldn't handle her.

K, is a savage because it's what her father made her. The only downfall she had, was me at one time, which is why me and her mother, get into it all the time. She always told K. not to let a nigga bring her down. It's easy for someone to say, when they're not in the situation. Her mom was the last person to talk shit, with all the cheating her husband did. It's always the ones who try to hide what they've been through and make their life appear to be better than others, that wanna give advice.

119

"Now, are there any questions?" Everyone said no.

"On to other news. Javier, is lurking somewhere and it's up to us, to find him first."

"What does he want?" One of the guys asked.

"My organization. Evidently, him and my father were in business together years ago and both retired at the same time. Unfortunately, B-Huff linked up with him for some reason and practically begged him to come back. He felt if Javier came back, he would get his product cheaper and become the king of these streets."

"Wait! So, this motherfucker wants back in?" I yelled. This Javier nigga had shit twisted. Once you get out, that's it.

"Yes Misfit. He feels my father should've let it go, like he did. Also. He isn't happy with my father's replacement." She pointed to herself and Shafee. He didn't do half of what K did, but they are siblings and she always told everyone, they were one. She finished explaining everything to her employees and told them to stay alert. I pulled her to the side.

"You know this makes you a target?"

"I'm aware."

120

"K, this isn't a game. You almost died." I was pissed she had a smirk on her face.

"And I didn't. Lucky for me, he only told Zander to cripple me. As of right now, he still thinks, I'm out of business and we're gonna keep it that way."

"K, I'm not sure about this." She patted me on the face.

"Misfit, you have a new woman to worry about now. I'm gonna be fine." She turned to leave and I snatched her by the arm.

"K. You will always be my concern too. My daughter loves you and I'm not about to let you be crazy in these streets and she lose you."

"Misfit, you're not gonna lose me and neither is Angel. Zander and I, may not be together but he's not gonna allow anything to happen either. Plus, he's going to kill Javier."

"WHAT?"

"Look Misfit. Here's a quick breakdown and then I have to go. The movers are at the condo to pack it up."

"Condo?" She started explaining how she purchased one to throw Zander off and I just shook my head. No wonder, he didn't want any parts of her, she was deceptive as fuck.

"Anyway. He feels Javier set him up and let's just say, he's gonna make sure he pays, for making him shoot me and us losing a child." I let her go and watched as she strolled out the place without a care in the world. *FUCK!* I forgot to tell her to take the hit off Krista.

Unique

"Hello." I said when I picked my phone up.

"Come open the door." He said and disconnected the call. At first, I was gonna let his ass sit outside but being I missed him, I decided against it.

It was after nine and Angel was in bed asleep. Yea, she's been staying here, since her father got in her ass. Call me childish, but I laughed my ass off when Carrie told me Misfit beat her. My child was so spoiled and he was the main cause of it.

On my way down the stairs, I thought about how he wouldn't speak to me for weeks and now all of a sudden, he's here. I could be petty but he isn't gonna allow me to be a brat in front of him. I looked at myself in the mirror, fixed my clothes and pushed my hair back a little.

I opened the door and bit down on my lip. Zander, looked so damn good, all I could do was stare. He wore some dark blue jeans, with a pair of retro Jordan's. His black shirt showed off his muscles and a bitch was damn near, creaming in her panties. He chuckled and moved past me. I started to ask, who told him to enter but if you saw what I did, there would be no questions. I closed the door and he walked up to lock it. This is his first time here, so when he grabbed my hand and led me up the steps, I was shocked. I pointed to my room and followed him inside.

"Come closer Unique." I made sure my bedroom door was locked and did like he asked.

"Did you miss me?" His hands were caressing my breasts, through my pajama shirt.

"Yes." I whispered and stood there as he removed my clothes. First, he kissed my belly, then moved down to my thighs, lifted one leg on his shoulder and dove right in. I had to keep my moans under control, so Angel wouldn't wake up. However, he made it extremely hard. Each time he sucked, bit down or flickered his tongue on my clit, a bitch went crazy.

"Yes Zander. Fuck yes." My body gave him exactly what he wanted. I caught my breath and pushed him back on the bed. I undid his jeans and watched my friend pop out his boxers. This man was blessed and I missed everything about him.

"Shit Unique." His hand was in my hair as I went to work, pleasing him. He may not like me being a brat but sexually, he let me do whatever I wanted, as long as it wasn't violating him.

"Yea ma. Fuckkk." He moaned and squirted in my mouth.

Instead of waiting for him to get aroused, my hands helped him out. I climbed on top and a bitch was in heaven. It had been so long since the two of us were intimate, every time I came down, it felt like he was ripping me apart. I turned to ride him cowgirl style and both of us were moaning out each other's name. He had me get on all fours and began fucking the hell outta me. I couldn't even get some of the moans out because it felt so damn good, I had no voice.

"We're getting married tomorrow." I heard him say and tried to move away but he had his hands on my shoulders, as he continued hitting it from the back and held me there.

"Zander. What? Oh my God, here I cum again."

"Shit, me too." Both of us released, he pulled out and got up. I laid there, until I heard the shower go on. He never told me to come in when he took one, but always said, it's never a time, I shouldn't be in there with him. *And he calls me spoiled.*

I pulled the glass door open and he was standing there naked, with a humungous, diamond in his hand. I covered my mouth and started crying. The entire time Misfit and I, were together, we spoke on marriage but he never proposed. Here, Zander and I, only known each other six months at the most and he's already asking for my hand in marriage. I stepped in and he got down on one knee. The water was hitting his back, yet, it didn't stop him.

"Unique, I know we haven't known one another a long time but what I feel for you is, as real, as it gets. Not only am I in love with you, I wanna have a family and grow old with you. I know, Angel is having a hard time but we'll get through it. I want you as my wife, as soon as possible, so what do you say? Will you marry me?" I just nodded my head yes and let more

126

tears fall. The ring was heavy on my finger but I'm not complaining.

"I love you so much Zander." I kissed him and we pleased one another again in the shower. After we got out, I looked down at my ring. I can't believe. I'll be Mrs. Zander Roberts in the morning. People are gonna be mad and I could care less.

****

"Bitch, I can't believe you're really going through with this." Ashanti said as we sat in the restaurant eating. I was able to get Zander to wait a couple days before we got married. I wanted to tell my family. My father wasn't too happy when he found out, Zander is the one who shot me. It wasn't stopping me from marrying him, but I still wanted to see where my parents' heads were at.

"Why not? I mean, we love each other."

"It's only been a few months." She put some food in her mouth.

"And? People get married within a week of meeting one another."

"What did my uncle say?"

"Bitch, I think he was more excited, than I was." He had Zander come over and by the end of the night, him and my dad, were so drunk, we ended up staying over there. My mom was hesitant at first but she wanted more grandkids and she knew Misfit and I weren't giving her anymore. Shafee, wouldn't dare sleep with a chick unprotected, so there were no grandkids coming from him either.

"And what about Misfit?" I turned to face her.

"Tan, Misfit and I, only co-parent Angel." She sucked her teeth.

"I'm serious. We had our chance and it didn't work out. He's in love with Krista and they're expecting." She let her mouth hit the floor.

"So, you're really over him?"

"I've been over him for a while. Yes, we still played around here and there, but once Zander and I, got together, Misfit and I, never went there again. He respects my relationship and I respect his, regardless, of what went down at the dinner. He wanted me to feel his woman out, and I can

128

admit, I got in my feelings, watching the way he loved on her. However, if she keeps him happy, then so be it."

"Well, I hope Mike is coming." She rubbed her belly and Elsie looked at her. She hated Ashanti; especially now that her and Champ are together and expecting. Yes, Champ and Ashanti are brother and sister. Shit, half the time, he couldn't stand her either, nor did he claim her.

"I'm telling you right now Ashanti, don't start no shit." Elsie shouted and she sucked her teeth.

"Why y'all worried about what I'm gonna do?" She smirked and got up to use the bathroom.

"I swear, Unique. I will kick her ass, pregnant and all, if she gets my man in some shit." I laughed.

She knew if Ashanti started some shit, the guys would jump in and since all of them are dangerous, it's no telling what would happen. I told her to calm down and think positive. Ashanti, may be spiteful but I don't think she'll do anything stupid, but then again, you never know. Oh well, I guess we'll see what happens, on my wedding day.

After we finished, Elsie and I went to Barneys, to shop a little more. Ashanti, claimed Mike was calling her, however, I noticed Andre's name pop up on the screen before she picked the phone up. Hey, if she's in denial, who am I to try and make her see shit for what it is? The chick is blinded and until Mike or his girl Gianna, knock some sense in her again, she won't learn.

****

"Baby, I have to pick Angel up." I tried to move away from Zander. Tomorrow, was our wedding day and I still had to get her a dress. She tried fighting me about not being in it, but I let her know, what was really up. I'm not Misfit, and will dig in her ass.

"You want me to come?" I looked up at him.

"What? I'm gonna have to meet her. Why not, do it today?"

"Zander, you do know, she doesn't like you or your sister."

"Unique, Angel is a child and of course, she's not comfortable with us, taking her parents away. You and Misfit, may not have lived together but in her eyes, you were still a couple. Actually, it's both of y'all fault, for trying to keep her in the dark about where the relationship stood."

"WHAT?" Now, I was getting pissed.

"You heard me. If you two weren't doing things in front of her, she wouldn't be the way she is."

"Zander."

"Don't Zander me. Unique, you two were still kissing in front of her, holding hands when you went out, calling each other all hours of the night and who knows what else. I'm telling you, she was probably confused. Then we come in, and BAM! You two are no longer a couple and my sister and I, broke up your relationship. By the way, take the hit off Krista." I sucked my teeth. I forgot one of the workers told me, who B-Huff's baby mother was. At first, it didn't make me no difference if she died. Then, I realized, she's his sister and Misfit's woman. Both of them would probably make attempts on my life, if she did.

"Wait a minute? Is that the only reason you asked me to marry you?"

"You bugging, Unique." He stood and started getting his clothes on.

"No, I'm not. Your sister has a kid by him, and you probably thought if we got married, she'd be safe." He chuckled and finished putting his clothes on.

"Fuck you Zander. I'm not doing shit." He ran up on me and pushed me against the wall.

"Let's get one thing straight, Unique, or K." His face was so close to mine, I could've kissed him, if I wanted.

"I'm not worried about anything happening to my sister. We both know, besides me, Misfit won't allow you, or any of those men you have working for you, to touch her. You can stand here talking all the shit you want, about why you think, I asked you to marry me but I know one fucking thing." I sucked my teeth and pushed him back but his grip was tight, so he was still in my face.

"I know you better have your ass, walking down that motherfucking aisle, tomorrow at three o'clock or I'll drag you, kicking and screaming." He placed a rough, yet, gentle kiss on my lips and left me standing there. I wanted to scream out,

132

there wouldn't be a wedding but he was out the door. Who does he think he is? I went to my window and looked out. He was just closing his car door. He looked up and blew me a kiss. I stuck my finger up at him and he laughed and pulled off. I ran over to the nightstand to pick up my phone.

"WHAT?" I shouted.

"You heard what I said Unique. Be there, or deal with my consequences."

"UGHHHHH!" I hung up and fell on the bed. I loved this man and him demanding shit, didn't do anything but turn me on. This marriage is gonna be one for the record books. I grabbed my phone again and made a call to Shafee.

"Hey sis. One more day." He laughed.

"Whatever. Where are you?"

"The office, why?"

"Shafee, I swear, you better not be fucking my secretary." He busted out laughing. If you don't know, my brother will fuck anything with a pussy.

"I just finished." He said confidently.

"I'm about to fire her ass."

133

"No, Miss. K, please. I swear, it won't happen again."
She yelled in the background, which meant, my childish ass
brother had her on speaker.

"Don't let it happen again. Anyway, Shafee, go in my
office for a minute." He told me to hold on. I heard him
shutting the door.

"What up?"

"Go in the system and send out a message, that the hit
is off on B-Huff's baby mama. If anyone even attempts, to
approach her or something happens, they will be killed and so
will their family."

I could've sent a message out from my own phone but
its not how we did things. The message leaving my computer
would be in code and no one could trace the number. Also, the
message automatically disappeared from the persons phone,
thirty seconds after its opened. Yea, we had all kinds of
crypted things going on in my organization. How the hell do
people think we lasted this long? It sure didn't come from fuck
ups.

"Say it ain't so." He snickered in the phone.

"What?"

"We've all been wondering, how long it was gonna take, for Zander to fuck you into submission and have the hit taken off." I was so mad, I yelled at him and hung up.

For some reason, they all liked Zander for me. They say he didn't let me get away with shit, and he's just what the doctor ordered. Little did they know, I'm the only one reaping the good benefits of him being mad because his pipe game, is worth the trouble, I get in with him.

Zander

"I can't believe you're getting married tomorrow."
Krista said. I was staying here with her and my nephew. She
told me, Misfit brought her here because of the shit with B-
Huff. I couldn't wait to see him and take his life. He should've
left well enough alone.

"I know right. Its soon, but sis, I'm telling you, she's
the one. Plus, do you really see her letting me be with anyone
else?" We both busted out laughing. Shit, after the stunt she
pulled with Chanelle and we were just having lunch, I can't
imagine what she'd do, if I did find someone else.

"Do you think, she's over Misfit?"

"Krista?"

"I'm not saying it to upset you, but we have to be extra
careful with them and.-" I stopped her in mid conversation.

"Sis, I think they're over one another. The dinner may
have been a wrong move, however, it showed both of them,
they could move on and be happy." She nodded.

"Don't be afraid to love him sis. He's already gone outta his way to prove, he doesn't want anyone else."

"But.-"

"Don't but me. If you think he's gonna cheat, then leave him alone. No man wants a woman, who won't trust them; especially when he hasn't done a thing to you."

"Fine! But if he does."

"I'm gone sis." I stood up and she jumped in front of me.

"Mommy, would be so happy right now, to see how far we've come."

"You wanna take a ride and see her?" I asked and she agreed.

My mother was a victim of AIDS. She contracted it through a blood transfusion, she needed from a car accident. The hospital was low on blood when she was brought in and used one that wasn't done being tested. Anyway, we didn't know it then but once she had it, we did extensive research on how she could've gotten it. See, my mom was a born again

Christian and had been celibate for years. It's not to say, she couldn't have been with someone but we knew my mom.

The lawyer had access to a lot of shit and come to find out, the hospital was in the process of testing the blood, before giving it to my mother. Because it was life or death, they used it. Not only did my mom get to sue the hospital for giving her the disease, they never informed her, once they found out, which, the judge said was neglect. The judge also said, she could've been saved, had they told her sooner. Unfortunately, even though my mom won a few millions, she didn't live long enough to enjoy it. Before she died, she placed half in my nephews account and the other in my name for when I had a child. She knew me or my sister wouldn't need it. She put some in our account too but I gave my portion to Krista.

Now, I'm standing over her grave with Krista and my dumb ass fiancé, has a gun to her head. Krista, had a few tears falling for my mom and didn't even notice her at first. I shook my head and put my hand over her arm and snatched her away. Unique was started to become obsessed and as much as I love her, I'll leave her ass if she ever pulls some shit like this again.

138

"What the fuck is wrong with you?" She rolled her eyes.

"Who the fuck is that?"

"My sister Unique." She covered her mouth.

"Zander, I'm sorry."

"Unique, if this is gonna work, you have to trust me or we're not gonna make it."

"Why is her hair different and she isn't as tiny as she used to be." I looked over at Krista putting flowers down.

"She changed her hair color when you put a hit on her. As far as, her not being tiny; you do know she's pregnant, right? Therefore, she would gain weight." Unique sucked her teeth.

"Is the hit off of her?" I moved the hair away from her face. I could tell she was in her feelings because I called her out.

"Yes. I did it when you left. No one is to touch her." She put her arms around my neck.

"Zander, I know you're not him and I don't want you to think, it's the way, I am. Right now, I don't trust anyone;

woman or man. I know you could care less, but I do have people watching you." I sucked my teeth.

"Baby, you're my man and will be a target too. When they called about you being with another woman, yea, I was a tad bit jealous but then again, nervous, that Javier sent someone to seduce you. I know you won't ever disrespect me but I don't ever want to get caught slipping." I had to smile. Even though, she pissed me off, I understood.

"Next time, call me first and let me tell you. There was no need to come out here for that." I kissed her lips and had her walk over to where my sister was.

"Krista." She turned around and her face turned up.

"Krista, this is Unique, my fiancé and Unique, this is my sister, Krista." They looked at me like I was crazy.

"I'm formally introducing you. The dinner was a nightmare and whether you two like each other or not, we'll all be connected, soon."

"I apologize Krista, for the way I treated you. Misfit, wanted me to feel you out and once I saw the way he loved you, I was upset."

"But why?"

"It had nothing to do with you but more with, why he couldn't love me the way he loved you. I guess, seeing him with someone for the first time, it threw me. We've never been with anyone outside of each other. Again, I apologize. Plus, your brother definitely gives me all the love I need and more."

"Apology accepted. However, I want to talk about Angel." I shook my head,

"What did she do now?"

"Nothing. Do you think we're moving too fast for her?"

"Krista, if we wait on Angel, Misfit and I, will never be with anyone. Your brother had to make me see things for what they are. She's used to seeing her parents, pretend to be a couple in front of her; only to see us with someone else. I actually had a talk with her and hopefully, she understands. I do want you to know, she got in trouble for smacking you." Krista tried to speak.

"I don't play that shit and just because her father spoils her doesn't mean, I won't get in her ass."

"Ummm ok. Is it ok, if I bring my son home?"

"I can't tell you what to do, but if I were you, I wouldn't."

"Huh?"

"I may have called a hit off of you, however, Javier is trying really hard to get you."

"Me?"

"Yes you. He knows, how close my team is. There's no way, he'd get to me, and unfortunately, he found out how Misfit feels about you. He thinks, if you're in his custody, Misfit will have me, cave in and give him my organization. We go hard for one another Krista, regardless, if we're not getting along. He knows this and is trying his hand at everything." Krista nodded her head and said she would wait for me in the car.

"You're not gonna be able to walk for a few days, so I suggest you get everything done today."

"Zanderrrrrrrr." I threw my head back laughing.

"You're cuter when you whine." I kissed her neck.

"I said sorry."

"Ok and you need to learn to trust me." I lifted her head.

"I know you're spoiled and used to getting your way. I don't and won't ever have a problem spoiling you, but when you go overboard, I'm gonna let it be known, if I'm not feeling it. Unique, you should already know, I'd do anything for you."

"I do but.-"

"But nothing. It's a difference from being spoiled and childish. I can deal with spoiled but being childish, I can't. Now, take your ass to do whatever you need to and meet me at the altar. Don't make me wait too long." She started to walk away and turned around.

"Maybe, I'll make you wait an hour or two."

"As long as you'll still come down that aisle, I'll wait for you." I winked and saw the biggest smile grace her face. I loved that brat and couldn't wait to give her my last name. Shit, I most likely got her pregnant again, anyway.

"So, you're getting married for real?" Krista questioned when I got in the car.

"Yup. And my nephew better be there as the ring bearer."

"But she said."

"Krista, do you think any of us will let anything happen to him, if we're all there? Misfit, can drive with you to pick him up and bring him back, but he shouldn't miss it." She nodded and left the subject alone.

****

"Why the hell did she have to ask for bowties? I hate these things." I complained to Mike in the room. We were at Unique's parents house getting ready.

Shit, if I thought Misfit or even Unique's house was huge, it had nothing on her parents. It was like a damn estate. Her mom had tents put up in the back yard, with ice sculptures, mad wedding decorations and other shit. The reception was in a different tent across the lawn, that had a walkway leading to it. I asked Unique why so much, she said, this is their daughter's wedding and no expense is to be spared. I understood, but damn. I offered to give them the money but her father cursed me out for being disrespectful.

"Man, I don't know. Gia better not even try it." We both started laughing. Gia has become a bridezilla, so he says. Krista said she wants the perfect wedding, since this will be her only one. I'm still wondering how Unique and her parents pulled this extravagant one off, in a week. I guess, when you have money, anything is possible.

"What up?" Misfit said, walking in with Shafee and Unique's cousin, Champ.

"Getting ready to throw in my playa's card."

"I hear ya. But check this out." All of us stopped talking.

"Would you be upset, if I asked Krista to marry me?"

"Oh shit bro." Shafee and Champ said at the same time.

"What?"

"Nigga, you always said you'll never get married. My sister, couldn't even get you down on one knee." Misfit waved his hand at him.

"Why would we be mad? Unless, you're doing it because Unique is." Mike said and folded his arms.

"Nah. I've been thinking about marrying her since the first time, we met. It wasn't love at first sight, but after the dates and finding out the type of person she is, I knew she was the one."

145

"Your ass strung the fuck out." Champ yelled out and we all busted out laughing. They kept clowning him.

"She loves you Misfit. I don't think she'd be happy, if we told you not to propose anyway. Just know, she won't play any cheating games and she's not as naïve as people think. There's an evil side to Krista and you witnessed some of it, at the dinner." He nodded.

"Just keep her and my nephew safe, and you have my blessing." Mike told him and they gave each other a hug.

"I feel the same. She's gonna want her own moment, so if you were thinking about doing it today or even later tonight, don't. Wait a few days and then do it. Krista, is always worried about others and wouldn't want anyone to think she's trying to steal their shine."

"Got it." He pulled this fat ass ring out his pocket.

"DAMNNNNNNNN!" We all yelled at the same time. The shit was just as big as the one, Mike and I, got our women.

"Don't be surprised if she asks you to return it."

"Huh? Why would she do that?"

"Krista is simple. She'll think it's too much but just say, her mom would want a man to give her something like that."

"You sure, I should bring up your mom?" Krista must've told him about our mom's passing in order for him to ask that.

"Positive. She says my mom is looking down at her all the time."

"Oh, and tell her its non-refundable." Mike added. We heard someone knocking at the door.

"Let's have a smoke before this wedding." Unique's father said coming in and closing the door behind him. He handed each of us a cigar and lit them. None of us, smoked them but in respect for him, we did. Not too long after, her mom came in and cursed us out for smoking in the house. Her father is a piece of work but her mom ain't nothing to fuck with, either.

There was another knock at the door and in walked Angel, Misfit's daughter. She came straight to me and everyone walked to other side of the room. Her father kept a watchful eye on her, where I kneeled down to be face to face, with her.

"Mr. Zander, I came to say sorry for the way I treated you. I wanted my mommy and daddy to be together. But I see now, my mommy loves you and my daddy loves Ms. Krista."

"Angel, I understand and accept your apology." She gave me a hug.

"Are you gonna give my mom a baby too?"

"I hope so." She smiled and told me good. Now she could boss around two baby brothers or sisters. When she walked out, the guys and I, went to the back. It was now after three and time to get this party going. Of course, we stood out there for another twenty minutes, before the music started for her to come out and when she did. As most men would, a nigga lost his breath by how beautiful she looked. I could see Misfit smile at her. Too bad, he missed out on what was about to be the best day of my life.

Unique

"Calm down child." My mom was fanning me. I was so excited to be marrying Zander, I couldn't stop the butterflies in my stomach or my nerves from acting up.

"I'm trying."

"Can I come in?" We all turned around and Ashanti sucked her teeth. Krista snapped her neck and smirked.

"Ashanti, is it?" My cousin got up, being extra dramatic. She was only six months but the way she acted, you would've thought she was about to give birth. My mom already cursed her out twice before Krista walked in.

"Yea, why?"

"We don't know each other and I don't care to. You're having my brothers baby, well supposedly anyway." Elsie busted out laughing and I had to tell her to be quiet.

"His fiancé is here and she may be in a wheelchair at the moment, but I'm not. Pregnant and all, I will beat your face in, if you even think about doing anything to her." All of us smirked.

"Bitch, don't nobody wanna say anything to her."

"Bitch." Krista moved towards her and I stood up.

"You're lucky we're here for my other brother to marry his wife. Otherwise, someone would be calling 911, for you right now." Ashanti sucked her teeth and sat back down.

"Anyway Unique. I don't know if you already have something used, but I brought this for you." It was a beautiful watch with diamonds all around it.

"Krista, this is beautiful."

"I'm glad you like it. It was my mom's and I thought you should have it."

"Krista, I can't. What if you get married or wanna give it to your children?"

"My mom had a lot of jewelry and other things. Zander may not be a woman but you're going to be his wife. I'm sure he'll be ok with you having something of my mom's." She clamped it on my arm and it brought the diamonds I had on my dress, out. Yes, I had my gown made in Italy and rushed here. I paid a lot of money for it and they even put real diamonds on it. It may be over the top to some, but hey, you only get married once. I gave her a hug and watched her leave the room.

"Unique, that's gorgeous." Elsie said staring at it on my arm.

"I know. Shit, I may return it after the wedding."

"You most certainly will not." Ashanti said standing up.

"If you don't want it, hand it on over."

"Sit your stupid ass down somewhere. You have to be the dumbest person, I know." My mom said and Ashanti's mouth fell open.

"You're sitting in here trying to claim a gift from a woman who passed away. Her daughter wanted to make sure she felt like part of the family, by giving it to her. And you're trying to take it for your own selfish and money hungry ass reasons. Then you brought a man here, you know no one likes, to piss off Mike and his fiancé. I swear, if your mama didn't die a few years ago, I'd smack her, for giving birth to an evil bitch of a daughter. Get the fuck out." Ashanti had a few tears in her eyes, but she knew how my mom got down. She didn't play when it came to her kids.

"Ma, that was mean to bring up her mother."

"Forget that little bitch. I don't know why you invited her, when you know she's only here to start trouble." Elsie said and my mom agreed. I didn't say anything else and finished getting ready. It was now four o'clock and even though, I told Zander, I'd make him wait, it wasn't purposely. The lady doing my makeup took long on my face. It was well worth it though.

The back door opened and everyone began walking out. Zander's nephew came to the wedding and I had him and Angel walk down together. Of course, everyone loved them. When it was my turn, I didn't really have a specific song to walk to and stood there waiting to hear what he chose.

I see us in the park, strolling the summer days, of imaginings in my head, and words from my heart, told only to the wind, of even, without being said, I don't wanna bore you, with my troubles, yea, but there's' something about your love, that makes me weak and knocks me, off, my feet.

I told Zander to pick the song and he's a big Donell Jones fan, so to hear his version, of Knocks Me Off My Feet, didn't surprise me at all. My father, looped his arm in mine and everyone began to stand. I noticed Misfit standing behind Krista and both of them, had a grin on their face. The Gia chick was in a regular seat but the small wheelchair was next to her. On the other side, Ashanti sat next to Andre and the look on Mike's face definitely had hate all over it. I doubt it had anything to do with Ashanti but more of the way, Andre was staring at Gia. I nodded at a few of the guards, who were already aware of Andre being here. They were to make sure he didn't start any trouble.

Javier didn't know we found out Andre was his son and most likely, had him here spying. I'm not even angry, because all of them are going to get, exactly what they deserve. I finally laid eyes on my future husband and he had the biggest smile on his face. The closer I got, his few tears became visible and it only made cry harder. My dad stood there until the reverend asked who gave me away and placed my hand in Zander's. He wiped my eyes and I did the same for him. The ceremony started and the two of us recited our own vows. He definitely had me crying from his words.

After it was over, we all made our way to the other tent. The DJ announced us and we partied like crazy. Mike and Krista stood up and did a toast for us but Misfit, didn't seem to be happy. I made my way over to him and he hugged me but not without whispering something in my ear. I smiled and walked over to Zander, who was laughing and drinking with Mike and some of my guards. Yes, I gave them shifts to work the wedding and they were done and getting tore up.

"Can I steal my husband and his brother for a moment?" I pulled them away and into a corner.

"I can't wait to get you home." Zander whispered in my ear.

"Me either but it has to wait." He moved away.

"You need to get your nephew outta here, right now."

"WHAT?" They both shouted.

"Krista is in the house using the bathroom with Gia and doesn't know but B-Huff, is a few roads over. As of right now, he's alone but we can't take the chance of him ambushing the wedding. It will cause chaos and he may be able to get his hands on your nephew."

"Fuck this."

"Mike, please don't cause a scene."

"Why not? I'm over these motherfuckers." He loosened the bowtie.

"You're my brother in law now, which makes Gianna, my sister in law. Right now, besides your nephew, she is the next vulnerable one. If chaos does happen, she won't be able to run or escape as fast. I know for a fact, you don't want anything to happen to her." He ran his hand down his face.

"What should we do then?"

"At this very moment, two of my best female hitters are in the house with Krista and Gianna. They are placing them in a bullet proof truck and transporting them back to Krista's house, where they'll stay until you two get there or I tell them to leave. However, your nephew is upstairs asleep, and Misfit doesn't want your sister carrying him out because of her pregnancy. One of you need to get him and take him to the truck, so the girls can pull off."

"I thought you said they were gone."

"No, I said they will be transported to the house. They're waiting for someone to bring her son to him."

"Why didn't Misfit do it?"

"As we speak, him and a team are suiting up to go after B-Huff."

"Fuck!" Both of them took off running and left me standing there shaking my head. I just told them to get their nephew and neither of them, ran up the steps.

I went in the house and noticed Angel sitting on the couch with tears coming down her face. She didn't see me but I could tell by the way, she looked straight ahead, someone was in there with her. I didn't take any time removing the gun outta my garter belt and moving into the room. There were two men standing there, dressed in black, talking. I hated for my daughter to see what would happen next but no one was gonna hurt my child.

POW! POW! POW! POW! I continued letting shots off until both of their bodies dropped. I pulled out another gun from under the coffee table. My parents had weapons all through their house.

Angel came running over to me, and that's when I noticed the DJ stopped the music. People started running and outta nowhere, bullets began flying everywhere. Yea, I was pissed someone is ruining my wedding day, however, I'm Mrs. Roberts already and the reception was just about over anyway.

"Let's go." I snatched my daughters hand and had her ducking with me as we went up the steps.

"Shit." I whispered. There were a couple men standing outside one of the rooms. I could only assume; Krista's son was in there.

"Angel, stay right here. Whatever you do, don't move. Do you understand me?" She nodded her head yes. I stood at the top of the steps and began dropping bodies. Once I noticed, all the men on the floor, I yelled out for Angel to come to me on her knees. I didn't need her accidently getting hit. When she made it to me, I opened the bedroom door and Krista's son, was on the floor crying. I locked the door and ran over to him. He had blood coming from one of his legs. I looked and he was definitely hit.

"It hurts." He cried.

"You're gonna be ok honey."

"I don't wanna die."

"You're not."

"But people get shot on TV and die." He started crying harder, which made Angel cry. I went to one of the drawers and found a belt, to tie around his leg.

"Look at me. Both of you." They looked up.

"Neither of you are gonna die. If I have to take the bullets for you, I will."

"Mommy."

"Angel, I need you to call daddy on your cell phone and tell him, we're in room four, and one of us is hit." She had an iPhone, courtesy of her father. I was against it, and right now, I'm glad he didn't listen.

We've done so many drills at all our houses, and gave each room a number. The reason being, is so the person didn't have to search, room to room.

"Mommy, he's not answering." We heard loud banging at the door. And shooting could still be heard in the background.

"Brian honey." I spoke as low as possible.

"I'm gonna lift you up and place you in the closet." He didn't say anything and I could see him going in and out of consciousness. I stopped the bleeding but he must've bled a lot, before I got to him.

"Angel, try and keep him awake, without being loud ok." I closed the closet and pulled out the automatic rifle, my father had in his closet. I made sure it was loaded and waited for the person to kick the door open. I didn't even think about it being my husband or anyone else. They would've knocked first to make sure family wasn't in the room.

Once the door opened, one by one, I laid each one of them out. It wasn't until I heard Angel's phone ring, that I realized, no one else was coming in. I searched the room for it

159

and couldn't find it at first. The caller hung up but it rang back. I knew then, it was Misfit and had to hurry up and answer. I finally saw it under the bed and grabbed it.

"Misfit, we need to get lil Brian to the hospital. He was hit in the leg and he's losing consciousness."

"Fuck! We're coming in now." I hung up and lifted him out the closet. His eyes were closed and I began to panic. It's one thing to see grown people die, but kids aren't something, I'm used to seeing. I'm not saying he's dead but he is definitely on his way. I heard running up the steps and instantly became nervous, until I heard Zander calling my name.

"IN HERE!" I shouted and seconds later, him, Mike, Misfit, Champ, Shafee and others came in the room. Zander removed Brian from my arms and ran down the steps. Misfit snatched Angel up and Mike, held my hand on the way out. Bodies were spread out in the house, on the lawn, and in the streets. Javier, thinks this is over but as soon as I find out if Brian is ok, I'm gonna light his ass up.

Gianna

"Something's not right Gia." Krista said pacing in the living room. We were supposed to wait for the guys to bring both kids to us, but it never happened.

"Why do you say that?"

"I haven't heard from Mike, Zander or Misfit and my son, is still over there."

"LET'S GO!" One of the women yelled out. The big one picked me up and carried me out to the truck, while the other one grabbed my wheelchair up and locked the door behind Krista.

"Where are we going?" I asked because she was speeding.

"Don't ask questions. We'll be there shortly." Krista and I, looked at one another and shrugged our shoulders. I sent a message to Mike for the tenth time, asking if he were ok and it went unanswered. Ten minutes later, we were pulling up to a hospital. Its not the same hospital we've been to and the building was small as hell. I only knew what it was, because of the big H on the top of the building. Once we got out, we saw all the guys and Unique standing there, in her wedding dress, with what looked like blood on it. Krista instantly began to cry and shake.

"Krista, relax. We don't even know what happened yet." She wiped her eyes and walked over to the guys, well the woman pushed me over. You could tell Zander and Mike were crying by how red their eyes were.

"Is my son ok?" Krista asked and everyone put their head down.

"Don't do that Zander. Tell me right now, if he's ok." He pulled her in for a hug and took her inside. Mike pushed me in and no one said a word. Some guard stood in front of the door and opened it when we got closer. Krista's entire body froze. She wouldn't step over the threshold and I had no idea why.

"I can't go in there." I looked up at Mike and he had a few tears rolling down his face.

"Krista, you have to." Zander said. She backed up and ran out the front door. It was then, I saw what she did. I asked Mike to bring me closer.

"What happened to him?" I ran my hand down his face.

"Javier, had someone ambush the reception to try and get him or Krista."

"But why?"

"He knew, Unique was untouchable, so he sent a team in to attack. One of them shot lil man in leg."

"If he was only shot in the leg, why is he lying here, like this?" He was lying still on the stretcher and he had monitors and tubes on his body. There was even a face mask on him, to make sure he was receiving oxygen.

"He lost a lot of blood baby and slipped into a coma. Unique said he was shot when she got in there. He was on the floor, but she has no idea, if he fell and hit his head or what. There's a lot of swelling on his brain. They don't know if he's gonna wake up." Tears started to come down faster. He kneeled down in front of me.

"I know you're hurting but I need you to be strong for me." I nodded my head.

"Krista needs you."

"I don't know what to say."

"We need you to bring her in here. Maybe, if he hears her voice, it'll help him come back to us. Can you do that for me?"

"Mike."

"Gia, I'm not going to accept that he's gone. None of us are." I wiped my face and had him take me out there to her. She was in the truck screaming. Mike opened the door.

"Gia, tell me he's ok please." She reached out for me and Mike helped me in the truck. Zander and Misfit, got out and gave us privacy. We sat in there hugging and crying for a long time.

"Krista, look at me." Her head was in her knees.

"Sis, I can't imagine what you're going through. But what I do know is, lil man needs to hear your voice. He needs to know you're around and waiting for him to wake up."

"He's in a damn coma."

"HEY! Don't snap at me." She looked over at me.

"I'm sorry Gia. I just don't know how I can go in the room. I mean, he's just lying there."

"He's not dead Krista." She snapped her neck at me. I don't care how mad she was.

"I'm sure, it's hard to see him like that, but he's your son. He wants his mother next to him."

"But."

"KRISTA, GET YOUR ASS IN THERE WITH HIM RIGHT FUCKING NOW!" I shouted at her. If the roles were reversed, she'd do the same. I leaned over the best I could and opened the door.

"Gia, I can't."

"Zander, come take her inside." He came over to the truck and Krista just sat there.

"I'm coming too Krista. It takes me a little longer but I swear, I'll be right by your side." She smiled and hopped out the truck.

"Thank you, baby." Mike said and pulled me to the edge of the seat. I felt my bottom half reacting to his kiss.

165

"I can't wait to get inside you later." I smacked him on the arm.

"Mike, she's gonna need all the support she can get."

"That's exactly why you're her best friend. Come on." He helped me out and carried me in. He sat me on one of the chairs at the foot of lil man's stretcher. Zander was on one side of Krista and Misfit, on the other. I think everyone had tears coming down their face. No mother should ever witness their child, in a coma or hurt in any way.

****

"Baby, you need to eat." Misfit said and handed her a plate of food, Unique's mom brought. She arrived about an hour ago with food for everyone. She said her husband had someone remove the bodies from the house. I didn't even wanna know, so I asked no questions. She also said, they'd be staying at Unique's, until their house was renovated. She wanted everything re-done.

"I'm not hungry." She pushed the plate away.

"Everyone leave please." Misfit's mom had come in and placed all her belongings on a chair. All the guys left but myself, Unique and her mom.

"Krista." Carrie who is Misfit's mom called out to her and she kept her head down.

"KRISTA LOOK AT ME RIGHT NOW!" She yelled and all of us sat there quietly.

"I can't." Carried moved closer to her and basically yanked her head up.

"Stop this right now." Krista tried to move her hands off her face but she had a tight grip on it.

"Your son needs you."

"I can't do anything for him."

"You sound stupid." She pulled the covers off Brian and lifted the gown up over his leg.

"You see this?" Krista wiped her eyes.

"His dressing needs to be changed. Now do it. Then he needs to be washed up because you know these doctors didn't do it. After that, you need to lift his body up and work his limbs out. Move them around a little so he won't be stiff when he wakes up."

"If he wakes up." Krista mumbled but we all heard her.

"Little girl, you're about to make me hurt you."

"Stand your ass up and help my grandson." We all looked at her. She was claiming lil man and her and Misfit, weren't even married.

"That's right, I'm claiming him. No woman, who is with my son is gonna neglect him because he's in a coma. Get your ass up and do what I said, then you're going to eat this food, to feed my other grandbaby." Krista didn't say anything and started doing what she said. She cried the entire time but you also saw how careful and loving she was.

Once she finished doing everything and eating, Carrie had Misfit come take her home. She wanted her to change and bring clothes up there for both of them. Carrie said, he should be dressed everyday, as if he were going to wake up. She kissed his forehead and told him she'd be back.

I asked Mike to bring me home to do the same. I was still in the same clothes from earlier and wanted to lay in the bed for a few. Zander and Unique were going to change as well and left lil man, with Misfit's and Unique's mom. There were guards outside the room door and a ton of them outside the hospital. I swore, some were on the roof but I could be delusional, since I'm tired.

****

"Mike, I want to shower."

"Ok." He stood me up and helped me undress. Of course, his dick grew when all my clothes were removed. He reached in and started the shower.

"You know, you owe me, right?" I sucked my teeth. He stood me up and I held on the wall.

"Mmmmm. That feels good." He was placing kisses on my neck and his hands were massaging my breasts.

"You're pregnant, aren't you?" He asked and continued kissing on my body. *How did he know?*

"I'm not keeping it." He stopped kissing me and stared in my eyes.

"I promise you, if my child is sucked outta you, I'm gonna fucking kill you." He was serious and scary looking. He

169

snatched the sponge and washed himself up. He stepped out and left me in there. I washed up and called him to come get me. I knew he wouldn't leave me, but I hated to see him this angry and still have to assist me. It's not that I didn't want the baby, I was scared, something would happen to our child. Seeing lil man like that, I don't think, I'd be able to handle it and I was trying to avoid the heartache.

"Where are you going?" He was putting on his sneakers.

"Out."

"Let me guess. You're going to her."

"Her? Who the fuck is her?"

"Your fake ass baby mama." He chuckled.

"I don't want that bitch. And don't call her anything other than Ashanti. I'm not sure if that's my kid, therefore, she won't even get the title."

"How long have you known she's been back, Mike?" He froze and it gave me all the confirmation, I needed.

See, I had no idea she was around or even going to be at the wedding. It wasn't until, I saw his face turned up at the wedding and looked in the direction his eyes went. Sure

170

enough, she was sitting there with my abusive ass ex, who was staring at me. I rolled my eyes and never even mentioned a word to him. I asked if he were going to see her, because he must've thought I missed her. Ashanti never came to the reception and neither did Andre. Now, that I think about it, I wonder if they're together. I don't care but it would explain how he found out about Mike and I, in the first place. I sat there on the bed, waiting for him to answer.

"Gia." I put my hand up.

"How long Mike?"

"The night you were in the tub; she was at the gate." I felt the tears streaming down my face.

"You left me in the tub, knowing I couldn't move, so you could converse with the woman who tried to kill me? Are you fucking serious? Is she the one who had the credit card, you claimed was stolen?" He came to sit by me and I threw the remote at him.

"I thought something happened to you that night. I was hysterical crying and couldn't even save you, if I tried. You came in the house and lied straight to my face. How could you do me like that?"

"It was an accident. I opened the door for the food and saw headlights at the gate. I ran behind the house and up to the car. When she opened the door, I was surprised."

"So surprised, you left your helpless woman in the house. So surprised, you gave the bitch your black card." I pulled out the papers in my nightstand and tossed them at him.

"Yea, look at it. Those are charges to women stores. You gave her the card, with both of us on the account. It came in the mail, yesterday. I was gonna wait for you to come clean, but being you never were, I felt you should know, I know."

"Gia, I just didn't want you to kill her before the baby was born. I planned on telling you and giving you free range to kill her."

"Oh, it doesn't matter anymore because we're through." I moved my legs off the bed.

"Yea ok." I laughed at him.

"You can say that all you want. You can threaten me all you want. You can even lock me up for all I care. It's not going to make me stay with you." I picked my phone up and called my mom.

"Hey. Is everyone ok?" My parents went to the wedding but missed the reception because my dad wasn't feeling good.

"Yea. Umm can you and daddy come get me."

"What's wrong? Where's Mike?" I saw him sitting there with his head in his hands.

"I have no idea where he is. I'll be waiting downstairs."

"Gianna, you know I hate for you to slide down those steps."

"It's the only way, I can get the door opened. I'll see you soon." I hung up and pulled the wheelchair next to me. I wheeled it to the closet and pulled a large duffle bag out and put it on my lap. I felt Mike behind me and continued, as if he didn't matter. And before anyone thinks it, I'm not being dramatic. I told him not to lie, cheat or keep secrets from me and he did two outta the three.

"Gia, don't leave."

"I can't do this Mike. Once again, you hurt me."

173

"I'm sorry. I won't ever do it again." He was kneeling in front of me. I had to put my foot down and let him see, I wasn't playing. If I let him get away with it this time, who's to say it won't happen again?

"Move Mike." I tried to get passed and he held me there.

"What do you want me to do? You want me to kill her? Just don't leave."

"You don't get it Mike. It has nothing to do with me wanting her dead. Yes, I want her to suffer but all of this, has to do with you lying to the woman, you're supposed to love. A woman who is handicapped because of her? A woman, who can't even make love to her man, right now the way she wants because of her. I CAN'T FUCKING WALK BECAUSE OF HER MIKE! FUCK!" He put his head down.

"She took a lot more away from me then my legs." He looked at me, like he didn't understand.

"I terminated a baby because she lied about things she did with you. Yes, I didn't have to but why keep a child with a man, who lied to me, about something so small, as buying his

174

kid things he or she, would need? You haven't been honest with me for a very long time, and I just kept overlooking it because my heart was only beating for you. I can't take anymore, Mike. I'm tired. Please let me go." He stood up and sat on the bed.

I moved past him and put the brakes on, at the top of the stairs. I tossed the duffel bag down the steps and held on to the rail to stand. I slowly slid down to the ground and to the last step. I unlocked the door and sat there waiting for my parents, who came ten minutes later. My dad picked me up and my mom grabbed the bag. I looked up at the top of the stairs and Mike wasn't there. Its what's best anyway. I probably would've cried even more, if I'd seen him.

Krista

"He's gonna be fine, Krista." Misfit said and closed the door. After his mom went off on me and made me take care of my son, he brought me home to change and bring some stuff up to the hospital. It wasn't that I didn't wanna help my son, I was scared to touch him.

"How can you say that?" I removed my clothes and turned on the shower. He came in behind me and had me face him.

"First off.... I would never tell you anything to make you feel good... Second.... we have the best doctors out here, taking care of him. Trust me when I say, he's gonna be fine."

"Misfit, I wanna believe you."

"Krista, I brought you here because at this very moment, lil man is being placed in a chamber that will help reduce the swelling on his brain. After the process, and they run a MRI to make sure it went down; he will receive a medication through IV, to bring him outta the coma."

"WHAT?"

"The new technology out there is amazing and I've seen the chamber work already."

"How could you make the decision without me? You're not his parent." I saw him move away from me.

"Misfit." I tried to grab his arm and he snatched away and finished washing up. Once he stepped out, I stayed in longer, thinking about what he said. Is it possible, my son could wake up? I had so many questions and no answers. I hopped out and ran in the room to ask him and just that fast, he was gone. I hurried to get dressed and grabbed my phone. I noticed a text message.

My Misfit: *Krista, I love you to death and even though you're hurting, you should know, I would never overstep my boundaries. I informed your brother of the action we could take to help YOUR SON.* He capitalized it.

He said to go ahead and do it because you'd be asking too many questions, when he could be getting better. I didn't agree and it took him a few more times to say it, before I agreed. I don't know what you're going through but I do know,

I'm not about to kiss your ass or let you come for me. I'll see

you around. Oh, and if you don't know, we're through.

I wiped my face and fell back on the bed. I didn't mean

to snap on him and felt like shit for even doing it. However, the

fact is, neither him or Zander should've made the call, without

telling me. I was upset, yes, but I most likely, would've said

yes anyway. I grabbed my things and went in Brian's room to

gather him some clothes. Once I locked up and sat in my car, I

called up Gia.

"Hey you ok?" She asked. I could hear in her voice,

that something was wrong. I explained everything and she

sucked her teeth.

"Krista, he needed to leave."

"Huh?"

"Krista, he may not be Brian's father but trust and

believe, he has his best interest at heart. Do you really think,

him or Zander, would allow Brian to go in the chamber, if they

thought for one minute, something would go wrong?"

"I'm still the parent Gia."

"Yes, and you were mentally fucked up. They didn't want to put more on you than necessary. Then his mother had to basically bully you into getting it together. Only to have you go home and throw in Misfits face, that's he's not the father."

"Gia, I didn't mean it."

"It doesn't matter which way you meant it. The fact that you said it, speaks volumes to him, whether he admits it or not."

"What do you mean?"

"I mean, he knows he's not the father and don't need you or anyone else reminding him. He is at war with your son's father, over you. He was willing to go to war with Unique, over you. He is ready to murder anything moving, if they try and come for you. He's done so much for you and all I hear you do, is complain, complain, complain. I have to ask, what are you willing to do for him?" I didn't say anything.

"You're gonna lose him sis, if you already haven't."

"I'm not trying to. Let me go check on Brian and then maybe, I'll go see him. By the way, where's Mike? He's usually in the background talking shit."

179

"I don't know and I don't care." The sadness in her voice had me on alert. Did he cheat?

"What happened?" She started telling me and I felt so bad for not being able to go comfort her. I asked if she wanted to sit with me and she said tomorrow, she'd be up there.

I ended the call and pulled into the hospital. The guards opened the door and led me to a different room. There was a huge glass and you could see in a room, full of doctors. My son was coming out of this big machine and I saw a nurse injecting something in his IV. I stood there watching and praying, he would respond.

"He may not get up until tomorrow." I turned around and Misfit was sitting in the back corner. I was so engrossed in seeing them working on my son, I didn't notice he was there. I'm impressed he still came, even after the way he left. I made my way to him and sat in his lap. I thought he would move me but he didn't and I rested my head on his shoulder. I felt his arm wrap around my waist and pull my legs up.

"I love you Misfit and I'm sorry. It was never my intention to throw you not being his father in your face. I was upset, no one told me but I understand why." He wipes my eyes and moved my head to his.

"I know and it's why, I forgave you. I didn't mean to insinuate we're over because it's not happening."

"Then why'd you leave?"

"Brian doesn't know our mom's and if he woke up, I wanted to make sure he saw a familiar face." I stared at him. This man is perfect for me.

"You are the perfect man for me and I'm gonna mess up a lot. Please don't leave me."

"I won't. I'll just take it out on this pussy." He grabbed it through my jeans. We saw the lights go out in the room and walked over to the window. There was a small light on and I could see my son lying there.

"Can we go down there?"

"Yea." He grabbed my hand and led me to the room. I slid in the bed with my son and felt him place a blanket over us. It wasn't too much longer, when I found myself dozing off. He placed a kiss on my cheek and told me, he'd be back. He had to make some calls and wouldn't leave us alone.

181

"Goodnight Brian." I hugged him and fell right to sleep.

****

"Get up, ma." I heard.

"I'm tired bae." I could hear him laugh. I felt the bed, noticed it was empty and popped up.

"Hey mommy." My son said. He was sitting on Misfit's lap playing with his phone. I ran over to him and squeezed and kissed him over and over.

"Mommy, it hurts." He pointed to his leg that had a little blood coming out.

"Shit. Let me clean it." Misfit grabbed my hand.

"Relax baby." I stood there while, Zander lifted him up, placed him on the bed and let the nurse, clean the wound.

"When did he get up? How did everyone know he was awake? Why didn't you wake me?"

"Krista, you needed the rest, which is why, I took him out the room when he woke up. He kissed your cheek and said he wanted to play on his iPad. I called Zander and asked if he could bring it, and he must've told everyone."

"Thank you for everything Misfit. I don't know how to repay you." I wiped my eyes and went over to my son.

I stayed up under my son most of the day, while everyone else came and went. Around five, Carrie came and I asked if she could stay, so I could go home to shower. Once she said yes, Misfit and I, drove to the house. We didn't really say much, but I held his hand the entire way. Had it not been for him and my brother making the executive decision without me, my son may still be asleep.

"Krista, come here real quick." I heard Misfit yelling down the stairs. We got home and hopped straight in the shower. He hurried and got out before me and I paid it no mind. He may have forgiven me, but I'm sure it's still on his mind. I tossed the towel on the bed and threw my robe on.

"Misfit, where are you?" I shouted when I reached the bottom of the steps.

"In here." I followed his voice and covered my mouth, when I stepped in the dining room. He had a candlelight dinner, with roses and champagne. I noticed the music was playing softly and he was down on one knee. I know he's not about to do what, I think he is.

"Krista, you are by far, one of the most, fascinating women, I've ever met. You're about to have my baby and the way you hold it down in the bedroom, has a nigga strung the fuck out." I busted out laughing.

"I'm serious. I've never had a woman handle me, the way you do. I know, you're scared and nervous but so am I. But I'm willing to go the distance for you. Will you marry me?" When he opened the box, my mouth, literally hit the floor. The diamond was humungous and shining bright as hell.

"Yes. Oh my God Misfit. This ring is too big, and has to go back." I said staring at it, as he placed it on my hand.

"There are no refunds and wouldn't your mom, have liked to see something this big on your hand?" I stopped and looked at him. The way he mentioned my mom, made me cry and not because I'm upset, but because she's not here and its exactly, what she would've said.

I undid the belt to my robe and let it fall to the floor. He stayed on his knees and kissed my stomach, over and over. My

184

hand was on top of his head, rubbing it the way he liked. His hand, lifted my right leg over his shoulder and my fiancé took what is rightfully his. I tried to get away a few times but he wouldn't allow it. By the time he finished eating my pussy, all I wanted to do was go to sleep. However, he isn't about to let me. He laid back on the floor and I mounted him.

"Damn, I really love this pussy." He moaned out and sat up on his elbows to watch.

"And I really, love this dick. Mmmm. Yes baby." He pumped under me and a bitch came everywhere.

"You do know, if you weren't already pregnant, you would be tonight." I laughed as he flipped me over and placed my legs on his shoulders. He went so deep, I thought my uterus shifted. Of course, the two of us, went at it like rabbits. When we finished, showered and were on our way back, he had to carry me inside, because I was so tired.

"About time." Zander said. He looked at my hand.

"Oh, I see why now. Congratulations sis." He hugged me and I noticed a snarl on Unique's face. She fixed it when I got closer.

I gave Misfit a look, and he knew what it was because he took her out the room. I don't care what the fuck her problem is. I had my son alive and well, my brothers, my best friend and now my fiancé. I'm not about to let anyone bother me. I looked down at my phone. Except him. *Why the fuck is he calling me?*

Misfit

"What's up?" I asked Unique. I noticed her facial expression when she saw the ring on Krista's hand. Shit, I can't worry about if she'll be mad or wondering all the time, why I'm the nigga she wanted now, and not before. If I did that, I'd never be with anyone.

"You're getting married?" She had her arms folded.

"Yup." I lit a blunt and blew the smoke out.

"Tell me what's really good Unique? It can't be that, when you just got married yourself."

"I'm scared."

"Scared of what? That nigga loves you and do you really think, I'd be ok with you marrying someone, I thought couldn't keep you safe?"

"I don't know. What if he cheats on me? What if I can't give him any kids?" I noticed her crying and sent a message to Zander to get out here.

"Look, Unique. You're a beautiful woman and if you can't have kids, he doesn't seem like the type of guy, who'll leave you out to dry, over it."

"I know, but.-"

"Listen, you know, you can call me anytime but I'm with someone now and I can't have you making her uncomfortable because you're in your feelings about something." She nodded.

"We both know, Zander and Krista won't have a problem walking away from either of us, and neither of us want that."

"Yea. They aren't scared of us at all. Isn't that weird?"

"What's weird?" She turned around to see Zander standing there.

"How you and your sister, will leave at the drop of a dime."

"Well, its too bad, you have my last name now. I ain't letting you go." Unique smiled and I started to walk away.

"Thanks Misfit."

"Anytime." I kissed her cheek and headed inside to talk with Krista. She was talking to Gia, who had pulled up with her parents, while I was outside.

"Hey Misfit. I told Krista, she better get it together before you leave her ass." Krista was mad as hell.

"As long as, she keeps giving me that good, good; I ain't never leaving." I saw Gia smirk and Krista started blushing.

"Well, let me go see my nephew." She wheeled herself over to Brian and I noticed Mike standing on the side, staring at her. They must be going through something because she won't even acknowledge him.

"Baby, do you wanna take him home?" She turned around and stared at me.

"REALLY!" she shouted and her eyes became watery. I know she would cry a lot with the pregnancy but damn.

"Anything you want, you can have."

"There is a catch tho."

"What?" She was telling Brian he could leave.

"The two of you have to stay with me."

"Misfit."

"Krista, its for your own safety. After we get them, you can go home." She wrapped her arms around my neck.

"Baby, all I was gonna say was, you're my fiancé now, so of course, I'll stay with you." I had a huge smile on my face. This woman had a spell on me and didn't even know it.

"I do need to go to the house to grab us some clothes, his favorite toys and lock up. I may not be there, but that's the house, Zander brought my mom. I don't want anything to happen to it."

"Let's get you and lil man outta here. My mom will keep him at the house, while we go get y'all things and go from there. I'm gonna have some cameras installed tomorrow, so you can monitor the house."

"I love you so much baby." She and I engaged in an erotic kiss. Gia, yelled because she claimed no one wanted to see. Its crazy how Krista's brothers and I couldn't stand one another in the beginning and now we're all like one big family.

"You better because my ass ain't going nowhere. Now, let's get him ready."

190

"Uncle Mike." Brian yelled out as we were walking out.

"Yea."

"Mommy and Misfit are getting married. Are you and aunt Gia getting married too? I wanna be in your wedding as the best man." Mike looked at Gia, as her father pushed her and she rolled her eyes.

"YUP, we are and you can be the best man."

"MIKE! Why would you tell him that?" Gia yelled. Everyone got quiet.

"Because we are. You can be mad all you want right now, but we both know what it is." She waved him off but didn't debate anything he said. Women are not only a trip but hard as hell, trying to figure out.

****

"Baby, Brian called me the other day." Krista was putting clothes in a suitcase as she said it.

"I know." She stopped and looked at me.

"It's my job to know baby. You'll learn, you can't hide anything from me. Not even, that fat ass bank account you got."

191

"Yea, well, the money is for my son. My mom left it, from her lawsuit."

"He has his own account, Krista."

"What the hell? You know too much." I sat her down on the bed, next to me.

"Your mom left money in an account, for you to spend. Now, I get you wanna make sure your son is set for life but Krista, you need to start spending it."

"I don't want to."

"Why?" She laid her head on my shoulder.

"I feel like it's the last thing she gave me before passing. If I spend it, she'll be gone forever." I lifted her head and made her look at me.

"Krista, what I'm about to say may sound mean, but I'm gonna always be real with you." She nodded.

"Krista, your mom is gone." She blew her breath out.

"Baby, if there were a way to bring her back and have our doctors look at her, to see if they could've helped her, I would've done it, just so you could have her here. However, it's not possible and you have to deal with reality."

192

"I know."

"Baby, do you think your mom would want you being a couch potato?"

"I'm not a couch potato." She smacked me in the arm.

"You are Krista. You take hella good care of your son. You make sure I'm good, and you work your ass off but when have you done anything for yourself? Look at me." I lifted her face.

"I'm telling you to spend the money, so you can get out and see the world. I can bet my life, its why she left it to you. Krista, don't make your mom's death be in vain. Enjoy your life."

"What if I spend it all?"

"Your brothers will never allow you to be broke and you already know, what's mine is yours."

"You would give me money?"

"I'd give you the moon, if I could pull the bitch out the sky. Krista, I know he hurt you and you know what I did to Unique. But baby, I swear on everything, I won't do you wrong. Put the guard down and let me love you the way, you deserve."

"FINE!" She stood up.

"Well damn, don't be so excited."

"Oh baby, I'm sorry. I didn't mean it like that. I just meant to say, I do need to let the wall down. I deserved to be loved like any other woman. Right? Why should I shut you out, when all you've done is love me? You better not hurt me, or I may kill you." She kissed my lips.

"You better not hurt me, or I may kill you." She froze. I guess she knew, I was serious.

"You would kill me?"

"Get your stuff together, so we can go." I stood up.

"I'm not gonna kill you anytime soon, so relax." She let the breath she was holding in, out.

"You worry too much." I smacked her on the ass and went to the window. I saw some headlights pulling in her driveway.

"Who knew you were coming here?"

"No one why?" She asked and came to the window.

"Why is he here?"

"Who?"

"Brian."

"You sure that's him?" I questioned and pulled my phone out.

"Yea, that's his car. And who are all those people getting out the car? Misfit, look two more cars are behind him." She said and pointed.

"What's wrong." Unique answered.

"I'm at Krista's and we have company."

"How many vehicles?"

"3." We never said too much over the phone.

"On the way." She hung up and I put the phone in my pocket. Say what you want, but she and I, have a business relationship and if one of us were in trouble, we will always have the others back.

"Oh my God, Misfit. They have guns and.-"

"Shhhhhh." I put my finger to her lips and walked her to the closet.

"Listen to me." She started shaking.

195

"You have to calm down."

"What if?"

"You have my baby in your stomach and a son, at the house waiting for you. I need you to stay in this closet, all the way in the back and don't come out, unless you hear me call for you. Do you understand?"

"Yes. Misfit." She called out.

"Yea." I heard the door being kicked in.

"Please be careful. We need you." I smiled and covered her up with some clothes and shut the door. I tiptoed to the bedroom door and mad niggas were running through the house. I pulled the gun out my back and got ready for war. All of a sudden, I heard gunshots. It didn't take me long to get down the steps. Zander, Mike, Shafee, Champ and a bunch of other soldiers were laying niggas out.

"Did you see B-Huff?" All of them shook their head no.

"FUCK!" I ran back up the steps and sure enough, he was in the room with Krista in front of him. How the hell did he find her. He had a gun to her head, with a smile on his face.

"I bet you're wondering how I got up here, without you seeing." I smirked and waited for him to speak.

"See, this is her mom's place and believe it or not, when she wasn't here, I cased the place. It isn't many places to hide and being the first place, most women hide in, is the closet, it's where I looked, after checking under the bed and bathroom." *Is he stupid?* How he say, it's the first-place women run, but he checked elsewhere first?

"You ran down the steps and I was already checking the bedroom next door."

"Ok, you found her, now what?"

"Now, I'm gonna take my son and she's going with Javier."

"You're gonna sell your baby mama out, to a man you don't even know?"

"He won't touch her. He wants to use her to get you and Unique. Once we have the organization under our control, I'll be the King and you niggas, won't mean shit." He pointed to all the guys, who just ran in. We all laughed at him.

"Bro, let her go and I'll think about letting you leave." I still had my gun on him. He had a death grip on Krista and I couldn't take the chance of hitting her. I'd never forgive myself.

"Fuck you. Where's my son?"

"You mean the son, who was shot and in a coma?" Krista said, now pissed he mentioned her son. Somehow, she moved outta his grip and smacked the shit outta him.

"Bitch, what you mean he was shot?"

"When you interrupted my brother's reception, someone shot him. Now, you're over here demanding to take him and trying to get me to this Javier guy. I've always known you to be in some shit Brian, but you got us involved. Why? Did you hate me that much? Your son was almost killed because you're trying to be some fucking king. I hate you for this." She started banging on his chest and once he pushed her back, I fucking lost it on him. By the time, they pulled me off, this nigga was barely recognizable.

"I'll take it from here." We turned around and it was his brother, Riley.

"No, I wanna kill him." Krista said but I took her out the room.

"Misfit."

"No Krista."

"Why not? I wanna make sure he dies."

"He will but I won't allow you to take his life. Not because you don't deserve to, but because its not something you'll be able to handle. If you want pictures, then I'll get them for you, but you physically doing it, not gonna happen." She didn't say anything.

"Look. Your brothers are going with him." I pointed and Zander and Mike, were both walking behind some guys carrying him out.

"I'll have someone clean up over here. Let's get the rest of y'all stuff and go." My phone started ringing in my pocket.

"What up?"

"You two ok?"

"Yea. She's packing the rest of their things."

"Good. Listen, I have a meeting with Javier, set up. Zander, won't let me go alone as you can expect. Anyway, I'll

199

set up a meeting for all of us to discuss what's going to happen and we'll go from there."

"You got it. I'll call you later." I hung up and walked behind Krista to the car.

"He better die."

"He will." I closed the door and sent a message to Zander and let him know she wanted proof, he was dead. Once he confirmed it would happen, I drove off. This has been one hell of a week.

B-Huff

All I remember is going to my baby mama's house, having a gun to her head, and then things went from bad to worse. When I pushed Krista away to stop hitting me, this nigga, turned into a damn maniac. I'm no punk, but his hands were deadly and I should've been dead. Now, I'm sitting here in a room, with a bad headache, stomach pains, and it felt like my ribs were broken, cracked or something. I can't even tell you how long I've been here. I do see a tray of food on the floor untouched. There was a photo of my brother, in the newspaper for being a Kingpin, amongst other charges on the side of it. Why in the hell is it here? He's got a lifetime sentence, so I know its not him, who has me. This must be one of Javier's sick jokes, as usual. I swear, when I get outta here, I'm gonna take his life, grab my son and bounce. This shit ain't even worth it.

I tried to stand and almost fell over. I definitely had some broken bones. I made my way to the toilet and took a piss.

When I finished, I washed my hands in the little ass sink and glanced in the cracked mirror. My eyes were barely opened but I could see a little. My shit was fucked up. I lifted my shirt and there was a bone sticking out my side and blood drenched my clothes. Damn, this nigga didn't even have me cleaned up. I ran some water over my face to clean the blood off and heard some voices outside the door.

"I don't care how long, you keep him. I'll be here, until his spirit leaves his body." Why is Krista's brother here? Is he the one who has me in here?" I heard some keys rattling and made my way to the bed, as quickly as I could.

"Get your stupid ass up. We know you're awake, from the camera." I opened my eyes and couldn't believe my eyes. Not only did I see my brother standing in front of me, so was both of Krista's brothers and a guy standing, in a fireman suit.

"Hey Riley. When did you get out?" I said nervously.

My brother Riley, used to be the King of the streets, before he went to jail. Excuse me, before I sent him there. He had shit on lock and Unique's father was his supplier, which is why, I made an attempt to be with her. Her father, passed

202

everything down to her and I felt, we could run shit together; especially; with the beastly team, she had. Everyone was scared of them and that shit, intrigued the fuck outta me.

Anyway, my brother also had an empire but in a different area. My father gave it to him and he ran it the same way, my pops did. Everyone ate lovely but I wanted more. I went to Riley and asked if he could put me on as the leader or King in another area, so people could come to me. I wanted the same BOSS status my brother had, unfortunately, he told me no and I felt like he played me. Shit, just because my father gave it to him, he should've made me his partner.

Over time, I ended up gathering tons of information on him and handed it over to the FEDS. If he got locked up, at least the empire would be mine. However, when they took down my brother, they took everything with him. The organization dissolved and everyone started looking at me funny. It wasn't until, Riley informed the team, I was the one, who snitched.

Long story short, I met Krista and fell in love. She lived away from the drama and the two of us, started making money together. I mean, she went to school and worked her ass off. I explained my brother was knocked, the FEDS had all the money and I couldn't get it. She somehow handed me over five thousand dollars to get started and it was on from there, until I started to become greedier. Again, I wanted the same status my brother had. There were a few people working under me and I sold weight, which makes way more money, than the corner shit.

One day, I ran onto Javier by accident in a day spa. I knew the name but never the face. Him and Unique's pops ran the streets together and some say they had millions. All I saw, was dollar signs and introduced myself. It took a few meetings before he finally agreed, more money could be made. He planned on knocking Unique outta commission and giving me everything. Unfortunately, shit isn't working out, the way he claimed it would. My girl left me, my son was shot, I was shot a couple of times and I still don't have an empire or money.

"Surprised to see me, huh?" He pulled the chair up and sat in front of me.

"This is what's gonna happen."

"Don't you wanna know why I told on you?" I asked and he chuckled.

"I already know. You were jealous and did what you thought, would put you on top. How'd it work out for you?"

"Fuck you."

"You did bro. You fucked me with no Vaseline, when you snitched. You wanna know why, I didn't give you your own area to run shit?"

"As a matter of fact, I do."

"Because you were weak. As always, greed got in the way and you were slipping. Money came up short and you were just plain stupid and careless." He shrugged his shoulders.

"Now."

"Riley."

"I don't wanna hear shit. Tell us what Javier has planned and I'll put a shot to your dome, so you don't suffer."

"I ain't telling you shit. Shoot me." He laughed and called the guy in the fireman suit over.

"Nah bro. You're gonna suffer now." He smirked and the guy pulled a blowtorch out. He pressed it and the flame was super long.

"Yea ok." I called his bluff. Why did I do that? Riley nodded and the guy put the flame to my stomach.

"Ahhhhhhh." I screamed out, not caring, if I sounded like a bitch.

"Javier." Riley lit a cigar.

"Fuck you!" He nodded again and the guy lit the side of my head up. I could smell the skin melting and I'm sure, my right ear is completely gone.

"Ok. Make him stop." He put his hand out.

"He's setting up a meeting with Unique. The first meeting had to be canceled for some reason. He's gonna have snipers on each building, waiting to take her out. If Mike or Zander comes, he'll have people there for them too."

"WHAT?" Zander yelled.

"He's obsessed with her for some reason. She's all he talks about, which is why, he told you not to kill her. The shooting was supposed to make her angry with Misfit, for not protecting her. He was going to show up at the hospital to play it off and take all of them out."

"Where does he live?"

"Kill me. This shit is killing me." Riley nodded and the guy lit up one of my legs. I have never felt any pain like this.

"Ok. He has a house about twenty minutes away, from where the first meeting took place. It's the only house on the street and you will only see it in the daytime. He never uses the porch light and has these black shades and drapes in his house, to keep it dark and they're no street lights. Can you kill me now?"

"Nah. Have fun." He told the guy who shook his head. I don't know what happened after he burned my dick off because all I saw was black.

Ashanti

"Ok, Andre damn. I'm done." I told him after the last time we had sex. Don't get me wrong, I loved sex but I wanted Mike. Plus, he fucked up and called me, the bitch Gianna.

"Shut yo ass up. You have my kid in your stomach, so I can fuck, whenever I want."

"Nigga, we don't know that. It could be Mike's." I stood up to grab my clothes. Why didn't I pay more attention?

"Bitch, don't ever disrespect me." He backhanded me and I flew across the bed.

"Did you just smack me?"

"What you think? Get your ass the fuck up outta here and I'll call, when I want more pussy."

"Fuck you." He had the nerve to snicker.

"Oh, I did." He came to where I stood and lifted my face.

"Too bad, you're gonna die after you deliver. This pussy is pretty decent." He grabbed it and stuck his finger, deep inside. It was so rough, I know he touched my kids head.

"Yup, its gonna be a waste." He sucked on his finger and left me standing there. I hurried and put my clothes on, found some matches and lit his bed on fire. Fuck him. I'm gonna tell Mike what he did and see if he thinks, shit is funny then. I jumped in my car and sped off.

"What the fuck you calling my phone for? Did you deliver?" Mike barked in the phone.

"Mike, Andre, hit me and."

"Hold up. Andre, did what?" I smiled, listening to him sound concerned.

"He hit me and you know its not good for the baby." All of a sudden, I heard him laughing hysterically. I took the phone away from my ear, to make sure I wasn't bugging.

"Mike?"

"What? You thought, I'd come to your rescue. Bitch, are you crazy. You tried to fuck with him, thinking you were hurting my girl but now you see, exactly what she went

209

through. Oh, its gonna get much worse." He laughed and hung up in my ear. I thought about what he said and drove to my cousins' house. Yes, Andre put hands on me before but nothing this bad. A push here and there, and a few pops in the mouth. This smack is the worst, he's done thus far.

"What you doing here?" Zander asked when he opened the door. The two of them just got back from their short honeymoon. They only went to Miami for the weekend because of the shit going on here. They planned on going outta the country, when they found Andre's father.

"This is my cousins house, now move." I knew it was a low blow. Shit, he was the damn cable man and didn't have, nowhere near the money, my cousin had. But then again, he did do hits with Mike, so maybe he does. Oh well, the fact remains, this is my cousins house. I felt my hair being snatched and my body went with it.

"Bitch, I don't give a fuck whose house this is. You know she's my wife and you'll respect me. If you can't, I don't have a problem, sliding your ass across this room and out the door."

"UNIQUE!" I screamed out. His grip was deadly on my hair.

"Oh now, your tough ass wanna scream out for my wife. Keep talking shit, and no one will be able to save you." He said in my ear and pushed me away from him.

"Ashanti! What are you doing here?" *Why does everyone keep asking me that?*

"Andre, hit me and.-" She rolled her eyes.

"Why would you think he'd treat you any different than Gia?" *Gia?* Since when did she call her by the nickname? What am I missing?

"You're supposed to be on my side and what, are you best friends with her or something? I mean, you giving her nicknames and shit."

"If you haven't noticed, I married his brother, therefore, she's my sister in law." I knew they weren't blood brothers but damn, she is really defending her, like they blood sisters.

"Her and Mike aren't even married."

"Yet?"

211

"Yet, my ass. If I have anything to do with it, they won't ever get married."

"Ashanti, let me say this and then I'm done." I sucked my teeth.

"What?" I searched my photos to make sure, the ones of Andre kissing Gia, are still in there. I looked up at Unique and jealousy shot through my body. Not only did she have a beautiful pregnancy glow around her, she had everything, I desperately wanted. A house, a husband and so much money at her disposal, she could probably save it, for the next two lifetimes.

"You're infatuated and obsessed over Mike and its not good. All you're doing is bringing a baby, in this chaotic world of yours. You don't know who the father is and once you deliver, Mike and Gia, wants your head on a platter."

"Can't you do something about it?" She stared at me.

"I can but I'm not."

"What?" Just as I said that, in walked my brother and his stuck-up ass girlfriend, who is best friend with Unique and Zander. They all took a seat and looked at me.

"What the fuck is this, an intervention?"

"More like goodbye, because you'll be dead in a few weeks." Elsie said and gave me a fake smile.

"Chill babe." Champ said. I was mad, he didn't smack or tell her to shut the fuck up.

"Look sis." He came and sat by me.

"That nigga wants you dead for what you did to his girl."

"Oh, so you're gonna let him do it."

"Ashanti, you almost killed her and if it were me, I would've already taken your fucking head off, but I understand why he's waiting. I came over here to offer you a solution."

"And what's that?"

"I have a doctor who will induce you today. We can have the baby tested and send you away before Mike finds out. If the baby is in fact his, you won't have a choice but to hand it over."

"What?"

"Ashanti, you only kept this baby to spite him. Therefore, if you hand the kid over, he may spare you, as long

213

as you stay away. However, if the baby isn't his, then its best you never, ever come back. If you want the Andre dude to go with you, I'll handle it." I sucked my teeth.

"The clock is ticking, bitch. What's it gonna be?" Elsie yelled out.

"Fuck you."

"Fuck me bitch. You need to be thanking me."

"For what?"

"I'm the one who came up with this idea to save your trifling, ungrateful and ignorant ass but I see, it was the wrong move. You're sitting over there with your face turned up, when everyone in this room said, fuck it, let Mike get you because you brought this all on yourself." I looked around the room and all of them shrugged their shoulders. Was I hated that much?

"I'll take my chances on delivering without any help. Champ, I never thought, I'd see the day when you choose a bitch over your sister." Elsie stood up and tried charging at me. Zander held her back and Champ yoked me up by my shirt.

"You put yourself in this situation and wanna be mad at the world because no one wants to get involved. Sorry sis, but

214

you were warned, over and over to leave that woman alone, and you continued fucking with her and then put her in a wheelchair. You think a nigga gonna take kindly to someone hurting their woman? Then you talk shit to my fiancé because she's not about to let you get me, involved in some bullshit. Nah, it ain't going down like that. I love you to death sis, but ma, always told you, your mouth and promiscuous ways, were going to get you killed and I guess she was right." He was right, before my mom passed, she always mentioned how displeased she was, with my style of living. However, if she would've worked for my uncle, like my brother did. We would've had money and I wouldn't have, had to lie and scheme to live good. Shit, everyone knew how I was, now they wanna shut me out.

"What the fuck ever? Goodbye and I hope if he does kill me, it'll be on your conscious forever." Unique walked up to me.

"All of our conscious is clear, you know why?" I fixed my clothes.

"Because we warned you, to back off and you didn't listen. God, said you can't help people, who don't want help. All you can do is let them learn from their own mistakes."

"You changed Unique. You're becoming soft for that nigga." Why did I say that? She punched me so hard in the face, I fell against the wall. She kept hitting me, until Zander lifted her off.

"Unique, you know better."

"Fuck her Zander." She was breathing heavy.

"You have every right to be upset, but you're not gonna lose our baby over her. Call up the doctor and have him come over to check you. I'm not taking any chances."

"Ashanti, you selfish as fuck. How you talking shit, knowing how she'd react? You're gonna get exactly what you deserve." Elsie said and Champ basically pushed me out the door. Fuck everyone. Its just me and my baby now.

Mike

When Ashanti called, to inform me of Andre, laying hands on her, I had to laugh. Why did she even think, I'd care? I had no connection with the kid in her stomach. Not only that, the bitch made me lose my girl. Yea, it's my fault for not telling Gia the truth, but had Ashanti not kept the baby to spite her, none of this would be happening. My girl, had a lot of nerve, assuming we would be over. The day I proposed, we were already committed as one. Its about time to let her know. I gave her the space she needed and today, she was gonna give me, what I wanted.

Her mom and I, been working together, to make sure everything was right. Unique actually, let us use her house and at first, I said no but Zander, said it's the only way she could attend. She had three miscarriages and he didn't want to chance it, by having her leave the house and it happen again. I understood and since he was my brother, I obliged, on the strength of him.

Unique turned out to be cool but the reason I wasn't comfortable having it there, is because of her cousin. Ashanti is sneaky as fuck and she's the last person, I needed popping up. Zander, told me she came over there the other day and his wife had to beat her up. He was nervous because Unique was four and half months and the doctor said, for her, every month is critical, due to losses she suffered. He had the doctor come and check, to make sure she was ok.

"You ready, uncle Mike?" Brian said and put his shoes on. I smiled. Not too long ago, we swore he wouldn't be here but God had other plans for him. I don't think any of us, would've been able to move on, if he didn't make it.

"Yup and you're my best man, right?"

"Yup. Uncle Zander is mad at me."

"Why?"

"He said, he's supposed to be the best man." I had to laugh. Zander did ask, how I let his little ass, take his spot. Shit, at the time, I would've promised Brian anything, just because he came back to us.

"Don't worry. He'll be alright." He and I stepped out the room, looking fly as hell, if I must say so myself.

"Mike." Krista came walking towards me.

"What's wrong?"

"Well, it took me a long time to get her here. Anyway, she has been crying her eyes out. And." She was nervous as hell.

"Krista what's wrong?"

"Nothing. Never mind. You'll see, in a few. You look very handsome, young man." She bent down to kiss Brian on the cheek.

"Uncle Mike said, no dirty kid is going to be his best man. So, I couldn't play outside today."

"MIKE!" I shrugged my shoulders.

"You and I both know, soon as he steps out the door, he's like a dirt magnet and ain't nobody got time for all that." She started laughing and left us standing there.

We walked outside and Unique hooked the place up. I can't even describe what it looked like. Anyway, people started to arrive and I told everyone to make sure Ashanti didn't come in. If they saw her, they had my permission to shoot on sight. Baby or not, she wasn't about to mess anything up. Which reminds me, I need to have them look out for Andre too. Those two idiots definitely belonged together.

"I'm happy you're about to finally marry, my daughter. I couldn't ask for a better man, to take care of her." Her father said and patted me on the shoulder.

"Hey, cousin in law." I turned around and saw Precious. She's one of Gianna's cousins on her dad's side. We never said stepdad because it was informal and Gia would have a fit.

"What your nasty ass want?" I looked her up and down and shorty had a dress on, that was extremely short. She was pretty as hell but only looking for the next baller.

"Don't be like that. Shit, I did your future wife's makeup. The least you could do, is hook me up, with one of your sexy ass friends." Soon as she said that, Shafee walked in. I knew he was a nasty nigga and introduced the two. I left them standing there and took my spot in the front. The ceremony was supposed to begin fifteen minutes ago.

Ten minutes later, Zander told me the gates to the outside were locked. I appreciated no one being able to ruin our moment, and like the brother he is, he made sure of it. The music started to play and she had a few people walk down the aisle. I was shocked to see Angel as the flower girl. I didn't even know Unique and Gia, spoke like that. I know they're cordial but I missed out on a lot, in the last few weeks.

Don't wanna make a scene, I really don't care, if people stare at us, sometimes I think, I'm dreaming, I pinch myself to see if I'm awake or not,

Gotta be, by Jagged Edge played as the wedding song. Yes, I chose it. I noticed everyone stand up when the door opened. I fixed my tie and waited. The closer she got, the more I thought my eyes were playing tricks on me. Not only was she not in a wheelchair but she was walking without a walker. I swear, a nigga let the tears fall; especially, when I could see the pouch still in her belly. I didn't even wait for her to walk any further and walked to her.

221

"Mike, you're supposed to wait at the altar." I wiped the tears in her eyes.

"I waited too long for you." I placed my hand behind her head and kissed her, like it would be my last time laying eyes on her.

"Ummm. Can you let her go, so you can get married?" I heard in my ear.

"Nah, she's already my wife." I kissed her again and Zander finally pulled me away and walked me back down the aisle.

"And you call me nasty." Precious said loud and I gave her petty ass, the finger.

"Ok, then." The reverend said, once Gia made it to the altar. All I wanted to do was take her home and make love to her all night. I noticed her struggling a little to stand and asked for someone, to give up their chair for her. A few of the guys stood, but her father gave her his.

"We are gathered here today." The ceremony started and all I could do was stare at how beautiful she was.

"Is there anyone, who has any reason, on why these two shouldn't be married?" It was dead silence.

"Well, by the power, vested in me, I pronounce you husband and wife." I helped her stand back up and slipped my tongue in her mouth. It didn't take me long to lift her up in my arms and carry her outside. I didn't wanna disrespect my brother's house but I needed to feel her. I hit the alarm on my car and we got in the back seat.

"Give your husband a ride."

"Mike, I just started walking a few days ago and my legs are still fairly weak. Please don't get mad, if I can't do it long."

"Never baby." She pulled her dress up and revealed, she had no panties on. I shook my head laughing.

"I knew you'd want this after the wedding." I pulled my pants and boxers down and moaned out like a bitch, when she mounted me. I swear, she had the best pussy, I've ever had in my life.

"Shit, I'm finna cum Gia." We both laughed.

"Then let your wife feel you spray inside."

223

"Fuck. I love the shit outta you. Ahhhh." I let go and she screamed out, as she did the same.

"I'm sorry about not telling you Gia. You had every right to know she was lurking."

"Its in the past baby. Don't let it happen again." She kissed and sucked on my neck. I was becoming aroused again. We heard a knock at the window.

"Uncle Mike. What are you and aunt Gia doing? Mommy said, you should be inside."

"We coming. Get inside." Gia had her face in my neck, laughing. I moved her off my lap and reached over in the glove compartment for some napkins. After we wiped up, we stepped out and Krista, Unique and Precious were standing there, with arms folded.

"We in trouble?" I carried her on my back and moved right past them.

"Ugh ahh Mike. She needs to go in the bathroom, to change into another outfit, and obviously wash up."

"Whatever." I took her in the bathroom and stayed in there with her.

"Here are some washcloths, towels and her clothes are on the bed." Unique said when I opened the door. She had us in a room getting cleaned up. We ended up taking a shower first. I passed her the dress and had to stop myself from getting angry. It was white but short and sheer on the sides.

"Mike, I'm your wife now."

"Exactly! Don't you have something else to wear?"

"No. Its my day. Let's go." She took my hand and even though she could walk, I carried her bridal style to the area, Unique had set up for a reception. It was tons of people here and we had mad envelopes. Of course, Zander and Krista gave toasts and so did her father. When Precious walked up and asked to give one, I had to draw the line, because she had no filter. She had the nerve to get mad.

"You ready to go?" I asked Gia after we finished the last dance. We had our own dance, we danced with everyone who came, cut the cake and even had a soul train line going. I had to sit her down a few times but overall, we had a great time.

"Yea. I'm ready for you to make up all night." I smirked. Little did she know, it's exactly what I'm gonna do.

"Let's say goodbye to everyone and thank Unique and Zander." She nodded. After we said our goodbyes, I drove to the house and made love to my wife all night. She may have been weak but she rode my ass real good. I'm happy she's my wife because I'd be mad as hell, if anyone else received the same pleasure she gives me.

****

"Come on babe. I have a surprise for you. Well not really a surprise but you'll be happy." We had just come back from our vacation in the Bahamas. Its where she wanted to go. We did everything out there, when it came to tourists stuff.

"Where are we going? Mike, I'm tired."

"I know, but you'll enjoy this."

"Fine! But I'm not cooking tonight." She tossed the covers off her legs and stood up. I couldn't help but stare at her belly. I felt like it was getting bigger everyday. She was three months and I was excited. I tried to buy things already but she said not until she's six months.

We drove to the place her surprise was at, holding hands. I think we were both happy to be married and pushed all the drama behind us. The only issue we had, was Ashanti and her antics, of trying to get me to her house. I had a trick for her ass today though.

I parked in front of the building and Gia gave me a crazy look. It was the same place they had lil man at, when he was in a coma. I reassured her, that no one we knew, was inside or hurt. I waited for the guards to open the door and went straight to the room. I sat Gia down and pressed the intercom to let the doctors know, we were ready. At first, Gia had no idea what she was looking at because the table was covered.

"Did we miss it?" Champ and Elsie came in and so did, Misfit, Krista, Unique and Zander. Gia looked at me.

"What's going on?" She asked.

"Oh. We're about to watch the doctors cut Ashanti's baby out and then kill her with the lethal shit, jails use." I shrugged my shoulders.

"Mike."

227

"Don't Mike me. It has to be done. Now look. He's about to cut." The sheet was up, covering Ashanti's face, which is why, Gia had no idea, who she was looking at, when we first got here. Once they cut, we watched them do what was needed and removed the baby from her stomach. The nurse ran over to put the baby on the scale. I already gave them samples of my DNA, and they were getting some from the child. It was gonna take at less than two hours to get the results, because this facility is only used for the people in their organization. Therefore, lab work doesn't take the same amount of time, it would in a regular hospital.

"Is it yours Mike?" Precious came busting in with Shafee. I don't even wanna discuss how those fools ended up together. She had his ass sprung or something because Zander said, Unique told him, in the short time they've known one another, Shafee hasn't stepped out yet and he brings her everywhere. I'm not judging. Shit, my girl had me sprung before even getting the pussy.

"Precious?" Gia was ready to start asking mad questions. I told her to, hold off.

During the time we waited, I ordered food and we all sat there laughing and joking the entire time. Before we knew it, someone knocked on the door and asked to come in. It was the doctor who did the DNA test. I sat Gia on my lap and waited for him to speak.

"Mike, we ran the test four different times, as you requested and I'm sorry to tell you, but the baby isn't yours."

"YES! YES! YES!" Precious began jumping up and down.

"Thank you, Champ. Oh my God! I'm finally going to be a mommy." I could see Gia crying.

See, Precious was raped when she was younger and couldn't have kids. After the wedding, Shafee ran his mouth to her, about Ashanti having a kid and how I didn't want it, if it wasn't mine. She immediately called Unique and asked her to find out, if Ashanti would give the baby up for adoption and if she could be the one who adopted the child. Low and behold, Champ and Unique had her come over and sat her down. They explained she wouldn't keep the baby and if she really wanted it, she could be the mother. The reason she thanked Champ, is because it's his sisters baby and she thought, he'd want the kid. However, he was going to put it up for adoption anyway. He felt, at least if Precious kept the child, it would still be amongst the family.

I was happy as hell it wasn't my kid. I didn't cheat on Gia when she got pregnant but I would've felt bad having a kid by someone else.

After the doctor informed us, he took Precious out the room and like a sprung motherfucker, Shafee was right behind her. I told the other doctor in the room, it was time. He injected the serum in Ashanti's IV and we all watched her convulse, until she took her last breath. I though Champ would be upset, but he wasn't.

We all started to leave, when we ran into Precious who was sitting in the room, crying and holding the baby. Ashanti had a girl and once we looked at her, we knew she wasn't mine. The baby may have been newborn, but had none of my features. We asked what did she name her and the fool said Shafee named her, Heaven because it was God, who had them meet and now she had a kid of her own. Shit if they like it, I love it.

230

Unique

I was now six months pregnant with my son and out of the danger zone, as the doctor says. Zander was overly excited to not only learn, I would most likely go to a full delivery but finding out, he was having a son. Never mind the fact, Angel's bad ass, had him wrapped around her finger. I tried to tell him it's a scam but he didn't wanna listen. I'll wait for her to do some crazy shit and I bet he'll learn then.

Tomorrow is the day, to finally get Javier outta our hair. I called and set the meeting up and he was more than ready, to come see me. Zander told me, B-Huff said he was obsessed with me, but why? What the hell did he want from me, beside the empire? Its obvious, he was outta the game. And now, out of nowhere, he wants to get back in. I wanna say its him being greedy, like most men but he's as rich as, my father and shit, me too.

"You ready." I asked Zander. We were meeting Gia and Mike out for dinner. Krista and Misfit, were supposed to come but she wasn't feeling good. He picked Angel up and brought her over, to keep Brian company. Ever since the shit happened at my wedding, those two became best friends.

"Yea. Let's go." He took my hand in his and led the way out the door.

On the drive over, I pulled the visor down and checked to make sure my lip gloss was on. I put it back up and stared over at my husband. I really thought, I was gonna be alone forever or pine away for Misfit, to get it together. Zander came in my life at the right time and stole my heart away. Sometimes, I get up early, just to watch him sleep. He calls me a creep all the time and I mush him in the head. I loved this man with all that I had, if he ever cheated, I'd probably kill him, just so no one else could have him.

"Come on weirdo." He put the car in park and came to open the door for me.

"Why do I have to be a weirdo?"

"Ugh, you were staring at me the entire time. Only weirdos do that."

"Whatever." He closed the door and we walked inside. Gia and Mike, were already seated. They couldn't keep their hands off one another.

"Maybe, we should get another table, so they could fuck in this one." Zander said loud enough for them to hear.

"Shut yo ass up. Did you hear me say all that, when you were trying to get in Unique's throat, when you first came back from the honeymoon? Anytime I came over, you did the same thing."

"Whatever." Zander picked the menu up and used it to cover us from kissing.

"Nah man, cut that shit out." Mike snatched the menu from him.

After we ordered and ate, the guys wanted to have a few drinks, where Gia and I were ready to go. Both of us were pregnant and tired from all the food and desperately wanted to sleep. I excused myself to use the bathroom and heard Gia, do the same. I waited due to how slow she moved. Don't get me wrong, she was walking a lot better but she still had a long way to go. I give it to Mike tho. He never left her side and made sure, she felt secure in her spot.

"I don't know about you but I'm ready to have this baby already." I said coming out the stall. Gia didn't respond. With me being who I am, my instincts kicked in. The bathroom wasn't huge but the sink area, is separate from the toilets. I remembered my purse was at the table and had to think quick, in case she needed help. I stepped around the corner and sure enough, she was hemmed up, by Andre. How the hell did he know we were here or in the bathroom? He was whispering some shit to her.

"Andre!" I shouted and scared him. I walked closer.

"What the fuck you want? This has nothing to do with you."

"Come on Andre. Why do you have her hemmed up in the bathroom?"

"Because her man did something to Ashanti and now I can't find her. The bitch, is pregnant with my kid."

"Oh, you mean her husband."

"Husband?" He questioned and turned to look at me.

235

"Yea husband. And ugh, I hate to be the one to tell you but my cousin has met her fate."

"WHAT?" He yelled and Gia jumped. He let go of her and she slid over slowly, as I kept him engaged in conversation.

"See, she may have been my blood but she fucked over a lot of people. People who weren't going to forgive her and well, she lost her life behind it."

"Nah. Unique, you wouldn't let anyone kill your kin."

"You know, she thought the same thing." I smirked and lifted my arms to pull my hair down. Andre licked his lips and I knew then, he'd be too entertained by my body, that he wouldn't see me, about to take his life.

"Damn, Unique, you bad as hell." Gia was still in the corner, looking nervous as hell.

"Too bad you picked the wrong family member." I grabbed his shirt and pulled him close to me.

"Hell yea, I did."

"Too bad, you got caught slipping too." I used the hair pin to slice his throat. It's made out of metal and has a sharp edge to it. It could be used as a razor or knife, which is how, I was able to take this idiots life. I have to be extra careful, when I use it. See, I may not have a weapon on me but I will always be protected.

He grabbed his neck and blood spurted out, everywhere. I watched him fall to his knees and soon hit the floor. I looked at Gia and she thanked me for doing what she never could. I turned the sink on and attempted to get some of the blood off my shirt.

In the process, I asked Gia for her phone and made a call to Misfit. We needed to get the restaurant closed down and this mess outta here. I'm never this reckless but desperate times, call for desperate measures. Someone tried to come in but Gia blocked the door and told her, she vomited all over and was waiting for maintenance to clean it up.

"We need everyone to evacuate the building right away." I heard outside the door.

"Gia, we're gonna walk outta here, grabbed the guys and keep it moving."

"You have blood on your shirt." I looked down. It wasn't as bad as, I thought but it's still visible.

237

"I'll say it's ketchup. Let's go." I opened the door and people were running out the door. I noticed the two guys who followed us here, coming in. I nodded towards the bathroom and continued walking to the guys.

"Let's go."

"What the fuck happened?" Zander was on high alert.

"We'll discuss it, in the car." Mike lifted Gia up and rushed to their car. They knew if we were in a rush to leave, something was up. I don't even think they paid it no mind, that everyone else was leaving. Once we got in the car, Zander sped off, with Mike right behind us.

"You wanna tell me why blood is on your shirt?" I let my head rest on the seat and explained everything that went down in the bathroom.

"Unique, why didn't you come get one of us? Both of y'all are pregnant."

"There was no time. If I left her, he could've killed her. I had to handle it, right then. Zander, you know, I would never do anything to jeopardize our baby." He took my hand in his.

"I know. Is Gia ok? I mean, was she scared?"

238

"She was but she thanked me. I think she's happy he won't be around to bother her anymore."

"Unique, thanks for saving her. I know Mike would've lost his mind, if anything happened to her."

"Now all we have to do is get Javier and our lives will be peaceful."

"His time is coming tomorrow." He said and we drove the rest of the way home, in silence.

****

"Is everyone ready?" I asked in the meeting. Today, is the day, Javier took his last breath. My husband gave me a very hard time about even going. It took some persuasion from me and both, Misfit and Mike, to tell him, I'd be protected. He knew, I was capable of handling myself, but because of my pregnancy, he wasn't comfortable with the idea.

"Damn, you sexy, barking out orders." Zander whispered in my ear.

"Yea, well, you don't let me boss you around." I turned to look at him.

"Shit, I may let you now. Look, what you did." He pointed below and he was semi hard.

"Maybe, we should go in my office. I think, I can fix that."

"Not right now, you won't. Bro, calm your dick down. We got shit to do." Mike said and shoulder checked Zander.

"He stays, hating." We both laughed.

"Be careful baby." He lifted my face.

"I'll be watching." I nodded my head and kissed him before leaving. I thought about wearing the hoodie, but Javier's already aware of, why I wear it. Therefore, he'd have someone, shoot other places, like he did with Zander.

"Let's go." The driver pulled off and I looked back, to see Zander getting in a different vehicle. *All of this, will be over in less than an hour.* Is what, I kept telling myself as I rubbed my belly.

The driver parked outside the restaurant and came around to open the door for me. I stepped out and instantly caught a bad vibe. Instead of looking straight up, I used my pocket mirror, to survey the area. I pretended to put more lip gloss on and spotted men, on almost every building, surrounding the restaurant. There were some in trucks and I'm sure, he had a few guards inside with him. There was no need to send out a message, as I watched, things beginning to unravel, just that quick.

"Hello, Javier." I stood behind the man, I've never seen. I knew exactly who he was, because of the two guards standing on the side of him. He should've been more incognito, but when you're dealing with an arrogant and egotistical man, he fears nothing. He turned to face me and dropped the cigar from his mouth. I mean, it literally fell out his mouth.

"DAMN! You're more beautiful up close." He wiped the ashes off his clothes.

Javier, was my father's age and it's like time stood still for him. His features were of a man, to be in his early forties and his body, was very nice. However, even if I weren't with Zander, he'd never be a man, I'd consider. His theory on woman being seen and not heard, isn't anything, I'm could rock with.

"Am I to remain standing, or do your people have a little common courtesy, to pull a chair out, for a little ole lady like me?" He looked at one of the guards and he hurried to pull my chair out.

"Is that better?"

"Much." I smiled at him and then, at what I noticed outside.

"Shall we eat, first?"

"Actually, my husband fed me very well, before this meeting. I'm strictly here, to listen to what you have to say."

"I understand." He started to explain how he didn't make plans to return but B-Huff, basically, talked him into it. I sat there, taking in his every word, until he asked me to step down and allow a real man, to handle this organization. I had to laugh, which only infuriated him.

"You know what? Maybe, I will have something to eat." He snapped his fingers and a waitress came over. I ordered a small piece of chocolate cake, with a glass of milk. Yea, the two go great together. Once she placed it in front of me, I winked and watched her remove the gun from her apron and lay both guards out.

"WHAT THE FUCK?" I put a piece of cake in my mouth.

"Mmmmm. Javier, this is some of the best cake, I ever had." I picked up my milk to take a sip.

"What's wrong, Javier?" I ate another piece.

"You think, you're slick, bitch."

"Tsk, tsk, tsk. Why do men always call women a bitch, when she does something he doesn't like?" I nodded and the waitress, walked away, like nothing happened. Like I knew he would, Javier picked his phone up and made a call. He spoke in Spanish, but I understood. I wasn't worried about the men, he told to swarm in.

"You know, I thought we'd work well together, K or Unique. But I see, you're a stubborn bitch. Too bad, you won't see how I run this shit."

"Is that a threat?"

"Its more than a threat. You see, I already had men waiting for you to try this bullshit." I glanced around and saw what had to be at least forty to fifty men walking in." I wiped my mouth with the napkin.

"And, I knew, you would cry like a baby, who couldn't get their way. You see, my husband and my team, have been waiting a long time for you."

"Is that so?"

"Its so." Zander said strolling in. He took a seat next to me and ate a piece of my cake.

"My son, has you eating a lot but I can't wait to eat that." I stopped him.

"Baby, don't forget we have company."

"Oh yea. You want me to do it, or do you want to?"

"I WANT TO!" We all turned around and Krista came strolling in, with Misfit.

"What is this, a family affair?"

"Yup." I saw Misfit nod and one by one, all of Javier's men started dropping like flies. None of them, even had time to try and get a weapon out.

The look of terror was written all over his face. He sat there, in disarray watching my team take them out. By the time, the shooting stopped, the only ones left standing, were us and him.

"See, the patrons, waitresses, waiters and even the maintenance people, working this restaurant, are all part of the Buffalo team. You picked the spot and I made sure to have everyone in place." He looked around and everyone was smiling at him.

"Oh, and don't forget Mike and Zander, are the best shooters you ever had. My husband may be here, but we couldn't let Mike miss out on the fun. He got rid of all your men on the rooftops, in the trucks and a few others, you had lurking around, like homeless people." I pointed to Mike walking in. He ran his hand down his face.

"You were blinded by greed, and like most men; you assumed a woman couldn't do anything, remotely as close to this." I waved my hand around the place.

"You retired a long time ago, with my father and should've stayed that way. Since you didn't, its only right to make sure, you don't try again, in a few more years, if the next motherfucker, comes to you, about returning."

"YOU FUCKING BITCH!" He shouted and Zander, had his hands around his throat. I put my hand on his arm.

"You promised Krista." He stopped and took a step back. We all backed away, except Misfit. He stood behind her.

"This is for messing up my families wedding, shooting my son and bringing us into the bullshit." She pulled the trigger and instead of her shooting him in the chest, she aimed for his head and emptied the entire clip. His face was nonexistent and his head, was hanging off his body.

"That is the one and only time, you'll kill anyone. Do you hear me?" Misfit said and grabbed the gun out her hand. All of us, were against her taking his life but after listening to the reasons why she wanted to, we all decided, she could do it, this one time.

"I'm ready to go home, so you can BOSS up on me." Zander whispered in my ear.

"Y'all are so nasty." Krista said.

"What? We didn't do anything." I out my hands up.

"Whatever. Misfit, you see what, I see?"

"Yup. That's Her Man and She's His Savage."

246

"And don't you forget it." I kissed my husband's lips.

"Let's go see the savage in you." Zander is definitely nasty as hell. We all walked out the place and headed for our own houses. Who knew, we would find true love, in people who had different lifestyles, from us? I do know, Zander is the only man, my heart beats for, well and my son. We're never getting divorced.

Epilogue

Misfit and Krista, finally had their wedding but

she wanted it in Aruba. She said, after Misfit talked her into

spending money, her mom left, she was gonna start by using it

towards the wedding. Little did she know. Misfit had already

replaced the money she used in another account.

They had a little girl, and named her Passion. They said

Angel, is the one who came up with it. I'm not sure why Krista

let her name the baby, but hey, if they like it, I love it.

Mike and Gianna, had a son, and I swear, Mike

was a big ass kid, when she delivered. He wouldn't let anyone

hold him and even told Gia, when he's not around, no one

better touch him. Krista and I, both had to sneak over there, in

order to hold him. He claims its because that's his first child

and no one is spoiling his son, but him. I hate to tell him, but

Gianna already has him spoiled. They moved into a house a he

built from the ground up because she refused to live in a house, he lied to her in. I could see if he cheated in there but I guess, we all have weird ways about ourselves.

Zander and Me, had our son and unfortunately, I'm the one who got pregnant, as soon as the doctor told me, we could have sex again. I swear, Zander did it on purpose. He always said, we were having a big family. He wasn't lying because between all of our kids, we had a hella big one. The dinners we have are always comical and the men always drink themselves to a stupor. However, the love we all had for each other, outweighs any hate, we had for one another in the past.

The End

Coming Soon

2017

A Dope Boy's

Seduction

Sneek peek!!

Mazza

"Put all your shit on the table." I said calmly, as the two idiots, who robbed my mom let the tears cascade down their face. They each placed a phone and keys down.

"Where's the money you took?"

"She didn't have any." I had to laugh. Who robs someone and doesn't get money, jewelry or something?

"Please don't kill us. We didn't know she was your mom and.-"

"There is no and. Whether she was my mother or not, why the fuck you out here robbing anyway? Your brother works for me. It's a shame, he's about to witness this." His brother Rome tried to put his head down and I made security keep it up. I placed his brothers hand on the table and came down hard with my custom-made machete.

"Got damn. That's fucking disgusting." My brother Fazza said.

Yes, we're twins and identical. The only way you could tell us apart, is by his eyes. He has one hazel and one blue. The shit is scary as hell if you ask me. We used to call him Crazy Eyes, back in the day and he hated it but guess what, he used that shit with the ladies, to this day. Those dumb bitches loved his ass too; even though he treated them like shit.

One time this nigga, had two girlfriends and all three of them lived together. It was every man's dream but it turned into a nightmare. Needless to say, the shit didn't work out because when he fucked one, the other, always got jealous. He'd have to break up fights, at least four times a week. Hey, if they let him do it, I ain't judging.

Now back to the situation at hand. The real reason, I chopped this kid hand off, isn't because he robbed my mother. To be honest, the lady wasn't even related to me but it was the principle. I'm a business man, who has a lot of money rolling in off the streets and didn't need the cops investigating a motherfucking thing. They start asking questions and volunteering information they shouldn't be, which will then, stop the cash flow and I can't have that going on.

"What's your name?" I asked the other kid who literally peed on himself.

"Lucky."

"LUCKY!" Me and my brother busted out laughing.

"Your ass ain't lucky today, my nigga." I took my gun out and shot him in the leg. None of the soldiers moved, not even Rome, whose brother hand, I chopped off.

"Listen here gentlemen. The moral to this story is; I allow all of you to eat very well. Therefore, none of your siblings should be robbing anyone. Now, some of you may think, you're the one standing on the corner, and you're the one staying up all night, so why should they get anything, and that may be true. However, your family should never, ever go without. If the bills are paid, food in the fridge and they have clothes on their back; there's no need to steal."

"Can I get a doctor please?" Lucky said. The other kid was barely keeping his eyes open, due to the amount of blood loss from his hand. I ignored him and kept talking, as if both of them weren't leaking blood all over my floor.

"There may be some knuckleheads running around but the reason most people steal, is because they're without something. Now, tell me what's missing in your house?" I lifted the kids head up.

"Food. We haven't had any for a week and the first isn't, until next Tuesday." He said and it only fueled my anger.

"Get them in the back to see the doctor." I kept one on call. See, I didn't kill too many people unless it's necessary. I did make sure to leave them with a constant memory of how not to fuck with me.

"ROME! FRONT AND MOTHERFUCKIN CENTER!" I yelled out to the kids' brother. He came towards me and I beat the shit outta him. I kneeled down and lifted his head.

"Never see your family without because you're trying to politic with the bitches. Pussy come and go but your family, will always have your back." I slammed his head in the ground.

"Let this be a lesson to all of you. Don't lose a family member, being greedy and selfish. If a nigga will steal from old people, he'll steal from you and there's no sympathy for someone who's late with my money." I picked the towel up and wiped down my machete.

"Ahhhhhhh." You heard someone scream out.

"Someone is gonna need a prosthetic." Fazza said laughing and walked to the back to see what was going on.

"Get this nigga off my floor and send one of those bitches from downstairs to suck my dick. I need to release myself ASAP."

The woman who worked here were always willing to fuck with me or my brother. Me, however, I used them for head and nothing else. I don't need no strung-out bitches on payroll. They get too messy and I'll kill a bitch whole family, for messing with my money.

I walked upstairs to one of the offices. Today has been a crazy day. I thought to myself when one of the regulars came in to give me exactly what I wanted. She was a bad one, but I stuck to my head only motto with these bitches. I don't trust no fucking body but my brother and its gonna stay that way.

"Hurry the fuck up. I got shit to do." She sucked her teeth but did what I said. This is the life! I laid back on the chair and let her suck all my kids out, more than once. If I wasn't fucking, the least she could do, is allow me to feel those tonsils a few times. I know, I ain't shit, but the bitches, can't get enough.

CPSIA information can be obtained
at www.ICGtesting.com
Printed in the USA
LVHW011657180119
604419LV00014B/587/P